The Sunflower Girl

By Holly Fox

The Sunflower Girl

Author: Holly Fox

Editing: Paige Lawson & Florence Williams

Cover Design and Illustrations: Saira Morgan

Please visit https://hollyfoxwrites.myshopify.com **for information on trigger warnings.**

To you,

...you are enough and more.

Playlist

"Heavy"- Orla Gartland

"All Too Well (Sad Girl Autumn Version)"- Taylor Swift

"Daylight – Live From Paris"- Taylor Swift

"Please Notice"- Christian Leave

"Godspeed"- James Blake

"Fade into You"- Mazzy Star

"Funeral"- Phoebe Bridgers

"Now & Then"- Lily Kershaw

"Turning Page"- Sydney Rose

"Nothing New (ft Phoebe Bridgers)"- Taylor Swift

"Repeat until Death"- Novo Amor

"Loving & Losing"- Delaney Bailey

"Falling"- Harry Styles

Louise Present Day

'I can't lose you,' he cried breathlessly, holding onto her limp body as the blood poured from the wound in her stomach. Pulling her closer, he looked into her eyes as the light that had once been so bright, faded away. Studying her, he wanted to capture her beauty, so he could remember her face for the rest of time. They would find her, then she would be safe, but he had to leave before they saw him. This was the last time it would ever be just the two of them. The war had begun, and so their love must end.'

I placed my keyboard back on the desk, toggled the mouse to the 'save file' button, opened my email and typed in my agent's name before attaching the 'Final draft' to the email.

From: Louise Moore

To: Kayleigh Anderson

Subject: Final Draft

IT'S DONE – TIME FOR A LARGE GLASS OF PINOT. SEE YOU IN 30 MINS.

Lou

I clicked send and closed down my computer whilst staring at the blank screen, taking in the moment.

My fingers traced the weathered ridges of my leather desk chair, changing course when I encountered a rip in the fabric. Maybe it was time to get a new chair with my advance money.

For the past few years, I constantly denied the idea that I was a real author…even with a published book. I'm not sure why. My body just couldn't help but reject the notion.

Whenever someone asked me what I did for a living, my brain would take control and I would go on to tell them

I was in administration. It was easier, less embarrassing, but I knew I couldn't deny it much longer—especially now that my second book was complete.

I should have probably started taking it more seriously, even if that just meant buying a better chair
that didn't creak every time I sat on it, leaving me with backache for a week.

It was a less than average chair, but then again, I was a less than average writer, writing a less than average book series, because that was fundamentally who I was in every aspect—average.

I was convinced that at some point everyone was going to realise that the success of my first book had been a fluke. However, I did feel a sense of relief that Kayleigh and the publishers had the copy and would get off my back.

Out of sight, out of mind.

I wrote the first book one autumn, almost ten years ago. At first, it was just for me. A cathartic passion project that I worked on from time to time whenever a creative flow hit. After years of tweaking, I knew I could either work in the coffee shop forever or take the risk. Eventually, after countless rejections and zero interest, Kayleigh Anderson walked into my life. I had all but given up on my dream—serving coffee was easier than trying to figure out a backup plan— an email notification popped up on my phone.

From: Kayleigh Anderson

To: Louise Moore

Subject: The Midnight Circle.

Hi Louise,

I just read your book in one sitting and cried so much! I'd love to set up a meeting. Let me know your availability for next week and we can set something up in regards to offering you representation.

Look forward to meeting you,

Kayleigh Anderson.

I had all but forgotten about the book. I'd given up on ever getting any interest, let alone getting it published.

Later I found out that this was the first book Kayleigh had

chosen and pitched herself; the book led to late nights, endless bottles of wine, shared secrets and an unbreakable bond. We very quickly went from professional associates to inseparable best friends. I had truly hit the jackpot.

Standing up from my chair and worked my way through the piles of clothes strewn across my room, looking for something that could pass off as clean. A black band tee was hanging on the end of my bed; it
smelt relatively fresh. A pair of blue mom jeans were crumpled on the bathroom floor from when I last took them off, so I grabbed those too.

I figured I should probably do some washing now that the book is finished. The flat had been neglected for the last few weeks.

My reflection stared back at me in the full-length mirror that was free-standing against the hallway wall. My dark brown hair was its usual mess, despite brushing it only 10 minutes ago.

Sigh.

I clipped half back off my face, hiding the frizz. Two curls fell on either side of my cheekbones. My eyes looked tired, which I had tried to hide with days of built- up mascara blended into a half-arsed attempt at a smoky eye.

Whatever. I was only meeting Kayleigh. Any hope I had to be remarkable looking had gone a long time ago. Perfectly, forgettably average and, to be honest, I didn't mind fading into the background. It had always suited me just fine.

Shoving my black platform converse over my odd socks, I headed out my apartment door, skipping down the stairs to the ground floor when I noticed a new rip on the thigh of my mom jeans.

Ugh, these were my favourite jeans.

I moved the fabric of the rip around to try and make it look intentional.

A warm wind enveloped me, as I left the apartment building; momentarily relieving me from the muggy august air.

It had just gone eight, and by the time I'd get to the bar, it would be quarter past. Only fifteen minutes late- an achievement if you ask me, as being on time was not my specialty.

Walking through the streets of Brixton, I inhaled the humid air, which felt somewhat alien after spending weeks hauled up in my tiny apartment finishing the book.

A rush of new-found appreciation washed over me. The noisy streets. The hustle and bustle of the workers enjoying afterwork drinks. Families pushing prams of sleeping children home from the park. Groups of friends meeting for alfresco dining on street corners. The buzz. It reminds me of why I'm here; why I love London.

Spotting Kayleigh's flaming red hair outside the bar where we had arranged to meet, I quickened my pace, excited to engage in a conversation with someone
other than myself.

Kayleigh was sitting on a wicker chair at one of the

outdoor tables, handing a bottle of champagne back to a young, nervous-looking waiter.

She glanced up and saw me approaching her, flashing me her wide, perfect smile. Standing up from her chair she came to embrace me. Her emerald green cowl neck dress, showed just the right amount of her perfectly round double-D breasts and was just short enough to skim the thighs of her long, lean legs.

“He brought the wrong champagne! I’m spoiling you tonight, none of the cheap stuff,” Kayleigh said as she greeted me. That was another thing I admired about Kayleigh. Her energy screamed CEO of ‘not giving a fuck’. Unapologetically telling people exactly how it was, the type of friend a CEO of ‘not making a fuss’ person like me needed.

“Does he not know you represent a two-time bestselling author? Get him fired immediately!"

“Ha ha,” she mocked as I stuck my tongue out. “I just want to celebrate properly. You deserve it, Lou.”

“Well, I couldn’t have done it without you.” I smiled at her as her eyes lit up with appreciation.

The waiter returned, interrupting our moment byplacing the ice bucket on the table. As I looked up at him, I noticed his eyes were fixed on Kayleigh as he nervously opened the bottle of Veuve Clicquot, his eyes were fixated on Kayleigh, looking for any signs of disapproval from her. His hands shook as he popped the cork off the bottle and carefully poured the pale bubbly liquid into two champagne flutes before placing the bottle into the ice.

"Can I get you anything else?" his voice quivered.

"Thank you, gorgeous, that's perfect," Kayleigh said, placing a hand on his forearm and winking.

That was the thing with Kayleigh, the way she put people in their place always left them seeking her validation after. People wanted her to like them, and, typically, people were putty in Kayleigh's hands. It was one of the many reasons she made such a fantastic agent.

The waiter left the table, blushing from Kayleigh's affection.

She immediately clocked me smirking at her. "Oh stop, you know I like the stupid ones. They're better in bed." We shared a laugh as we picked up our glasses. "Well, Miss Moore, to you, you talented little thing." We clinked glasses.

"And to you, you bossy little thing." returning her appreciation. I took a sip of the champagne, feeling the bubbles melt in my mouth. This wasn't the champagne I was used to, it tasted so smooth compared to the cheap stuff from the corner shop that left a sharp, bitter aftertaste and a pounding three-day headache.

"The editor is going to begin running over the final edit on Monday, and we should be getting the covers for approval in the next few weeks too," Kayleigh conversed, pulling me from my champagne daze.

"I hope they're happy with it. I'm not sure I can add any more," I said, shuffling in my seat awkwardly. I hated this part of the process, knowing people could tear apart my words so freely when, to me, each word had been so carefully chosen.

"Don't be silly, Lou, your last book did great, and this one's even better. Your fans have been calling out for a sequel. The publishers would be morons not to exploit that."

I nodded in response to Kayleigh. Now was *not* the time to express my concerns over a third book.

It's just… I knew I had a very loyal fan base—well, the books did. It was a story of two rival kingdoms, where the protagonists fall in love whilst fighting for
opposing sides. It was Romeo and Juliet meets Game of
Thrones, and (thanks to Twitter) had become a best-
seller among the young adult fantasy community. The publishers had asked for a trilogy shortly after seeing the online following 'The Midnight Circle' had gained.

But, in all honesty, I wasn't sure I had the third book in me. It had been hard enough
continuing the story for the second book, especially when it had been so long since I had written the
first. I had no experience in happy endings, so I wasn't sure I could fulfil the expectations of my readers.

"I'm going to fuck him tonight," Kayleigh's voice sliced through my thoughts.

I choked on my champagne, startled, and looked around to see Kayleigh smiling and waving flirtatiously towards the waiter. He blushed, trying to keep eye contact with her while serving the other customers.

"I do not doubt that." I laughed, kicking her under the table to get her attention back to me. Kayleigh had an appetite for sex with men, women and anyone she took a liking to. She was insatiable and found beauty in everyone and once she had her eye on someone, she was relentless.

She turned her attention from the waiter back towards me. "What about you, don't you think you could
do with a good shag? You'll end up a lonely spinster with
nothing but a cat and a vibrator for company if you're not careful." Her eyes narrowed in on me.

It was true. My sex life was virtually non-existent. The last guy I slept with was a random tinder date who only had one pillow on his double bed and a roommate who walked around the flat naked. Desperation and three jäger bombs meant I slept with him anyway, despite the obvious red flags. He sent me a text the following morning.

Last night was amazing. You are amazing. I'd love to see you again soon. X

I never replied. It's been five months since, so maybe it was time I started dating again.

"Yeah, probably," I replied, ripping up the cardboard coaster on the table.

"That's a sign of sexual frustration," Kayleigh joked,

grabbing my hand mid tear.

We spent the next hour talking through ideas for the third book, moaning about colleagues and concocting a plan to get the waiter into bed. We were on to our second bottle of champagne, and the warm buzz was filling my body and working its way up to my head.

"I need a wee. I'll be back in a few," I announced.

"Perfect but be as long as you can so I can try and get his number whilst you're gone." Kayleigh winked at me as we both laughed.

I walked away from the table, towards the bar entrance and stepped inside. My eyes needed to adjust to the darkness, contrasting from the bright summer evening outside. Glancing around the large room, looking for a sign for the toilets, spotting one in the back left corner of the room. I headed down the corridor to the ladies' room and closed the cubicle door behind me, when I sat down, my head started spinning, the champagne bubbling in my brain.

My hand was against the wall stabilising me, realising I was probably far more drunk than I thought. I smiled, stifling a laugh. It had been a long time since I'd been drunk.

The last few years had been the hardest of my life and hadn't allowed for much fun, but I was finally in a good place again. I had finished my book, had a stable income, lived in a flat I loved and had an amazing best friend.

Things were falling into place for me.

I pulled myself up and flushed the toilet, grabbing my bag and making my way to the sink to wash my hands and looked at my reflection in the mirror. The alcohol had put some colour on my cheeks and neck. A downside to my pale skin was the flush of red that took over any time I was embarrassed or upset or felt any emotion at all.

I looked slightly more dishevelled than I had earlier. The smoky eye was smudged just a bit too far down my cheek, the heat had caused my hair to frizz even more, and I had a champagne spill drying on my jeans. I rolled my eyes. It's a good job I didn't have a waiter I wanted to take home tonight. I dried my hands and exited the ladies, making my way back down the dark corridor towards the bar. I decided it was probably a good idea to grab a glass of water before I got too carried away.

I reached the bar and leaned on the large black marble counter as I waited for the bartender to finish serving the group of women next to me. He acknowledged me mouthing he would be with me in a minute. There was a rather extensive gin collection displayed along the back wall of the bar with endless bottles in various colours, most of which I had never heard of.

"Lou?" I felt a warm hand on my shoulder and a familiar voice penetrated my body, right through to my soul. My heart sank to my stomach. My head spun. A lump formed in my throat. My stomach clenched as if a bullet had hit me.

I knew that voice. I knew that touch.

I knew my life was about to change… again.

I turned around to face my past.

Louise 2012

"Oh, come on, Lou! You haven't come out with me in ages. PLEASE! I promise it won't be a wild one."

That was a lie. Going out with Maeve was always a wild one, normally resulting in me crawling into my room at four in the morning and waking up covered in sick.

"Do it for me," she pleaded.

I had to work the next day, but she was right, I hadn't been out in ages, and we only had a few months left together before we'd both be leaving for university.

"Okay, fine, I'll meet you at The Lion at nine. But Maeve, it *really* can't be a wild one."

"I promise, love you!" She hung up the phone. I opened my messages and began typing to my dad.

Going out into town tonight will be back late.

Lou x

I locked my phone and set it down on my bedside table. The phone screen lit up as I placed the charging cable into it, allowing me to catch the time.

Shit. I needed to start getting ready. I rolled out of bed and walked towards the bathroom, grabbing a towel off the banister on my way.

I passed Faye's bedroom and banged on the door. She was playing her new Katy Perry CD that she'd gotten for her birthday. When I got no response, I walked right in, opening the door to see the back of her long brown hair; her face was buried in a pillow. I grabbed her dishevelled orange Teddy that was as old as she was and threw it at her.

WHAT THE FUCK?!" She pulled her head up and threw one of her pillows back at me before reaching for her speaker, turning down the music.

"What the fuck' right back. What are you doing"? I replied, bewildered.

"I'm immersing myself in the music. It helps to get the full listening experience." She stared at me
impatiently, clearly waiting for me to explain why the hell
I was bothering her.

"Right, well, enjoy that. I'm going out at nine, so you'll be alone till Dad gets back from work."

"Fine. Now go away," she huffed dramatically. Faye was fourteen and in full teenager mode and enjoyed nothing more than being alone or with her friends. Mine and Dad's existence alone annoyed her.

Dad was working evening shifts all weekend. I was eighteen, so I was old enough to look after the house when he was at work. I didn't mind him not being there, and neither did Faye. I'm not sure Dad minded either. To be honest, I think he found it hard navigating two teenage girls on his own. He didn't always know how to talk to us, but he tried his best.

Closing the door behind me, I walked along the landing to the bathroom, the drones of music flowing through Faye's door. I turned on the shower and slipped off my dressing gown whilst the water heated up. My body stared at me in the floor-length mirror hung on the back of the door, turning my body to the side then front to ensure I could see all angles.

My stomach was round and bloated from my earlier binge. I knelt and hunched, headfirst over the
toilet, putting my fingers in my mouth towards the back of my throat until I felt the soft tissue of my tonsils. As my fingers pushed further and further, an involuntary cough began as I repeatedly gagged until a warm liquid came up my throat and out of my mouth, splashing as it hit the toilet water. I sat back to catch my breath, my eyes watering. It was disgusting, but the calm that followed made it all worth it.

Pulling myself back up as I caught my breath, I opened the door of the shower, letting the steam fill the room before stepping in. The scalding water poured over my skin, trickling over my face and onto my body. I lathered the coconut-scented body wash and smothered it all over my body before running my razor up the length of my legs. God knew how long it had been since I had last shaved. I only really saw Maeve, so there was hardly a need for it, but it was far too hot today to cover up my legs.

Stepping out of the shower, I stood in front of the sink, wiping the steam off the mirror with my towel; I grabbed my toothbrush and added the toothpaste, brushing away any evidence of my earlier sins. The water was dripping from my body and hair onto the tile floor. I would need to clean that up before Dad came back in case he slipped—he was normally half asleep when he got home from work.

I looked back in the mirror, this time examining my face, red and blotchy, brows wild, eyes permanently dark and heavy no matter how much sleep I got. My tiny B cup breasts stared back at me, they were so out of proportion with my wide hips and thighs. I knew I was skinny, especially after the four years of on and off purging, but my hips never seemed to change, they were always wide, and I despised the way they looked.

After rinsing my mouth, I grabbed a towel, cleared up the puddle of water off the floor, and returned to my bedroom before I could talk myself out of going.

My hair was blow-dried as straight as I could manage to de-frizz it. I picked up the hairspray dousing it throughout the lengths of my hair in a last-ditch effort to tame it. Faye had broken my straighteners last month, and I didn't want Dad to feel obliged to buy me a new pair, so I was holding off until my birthday.

I opened my wardrobe, working my way through an array of mostly black clothing, trying to find something to wear. A black cotton summer dress stoodout to me, and I reached for it and put it on over my head. It showed off my collar bones, one of the only parts of me I could bear to like but hid enough of my body to feel comfortable.

I took one last look in the mirror, rubbing in a spot of unblended foundation on my jawline, grabbed my bag and psyched myself up to leave the safety of my bedroom.

It was one of those perfect summer evenings that left a rich orange hue over the sky, making the bricks from the houses on the cul-de-sac even more vibrant. I began my walk through the housing estates towards the main road, greeting familiar faces I passed on my way—that was the thing with a small town like this, everyone knew each other and their business. I couldn't wait to leave one day.

The streets were quiet as I got closer to the centre of town, racing against the sunset. There was a small pub on the corner of a crossroad with white stone walls and contrasting black cladding. A sign hung off the wall, still from the lack of breeze in the air.

I made my way round the back to the terraced beer garden it was filling up with people spilling out of the pub. I walked inside, shyly pushing past the oblivious men who were too deep in beer to notice my attempt to get past.

"Lou, babe! Over here!" Maeve stood up from the table on

the far side of the pub, waving at me. The men at the bar turned around to look at her, but she didn't care. She never cared when people stared at her. She barely even noticed, but I did.

"Hey Maeve, you look great." I approached the table, hugging her before I sat. She did look great. She always looked great. I looked down and saw that she was in flats too, thank God.

"I got us a bottle of rosé," she proclaimed, pouring me a glass. She took a deep breath. "So, don't be mad, but a guy is coming to meet me."

I rolled my eyes. This wasn't the first time Maeve had coaxed me out under the pretence of a girl's night when it was actually just a cover for her meeting a guy.

"Who?" I knew this meant I would be stuck with whichever friend he decided to bring along for moral support.

"Alex Kennedy. You know that lanky guy a few years above us?" She was ferociously typing a message on her phone, transfixed on the screen.

"Okay, for you. I will suffer talking to another arsehole," I joked. At least it meant I would be getting my drinks bought for me.

She put her phone down and looked me in the eye. "You're the best." She grabbed my hand and planted a kiss on it firmly.

I turned around to see if there was anyone we knew out. A group of young men were staring at our table, looking at Maeve and gesturing, no doubt debating which one was going to ask for her number.

It wasn't unusual for Maeve to have a man admiring her. It

happened wherever we went: at the bar, in a shop, getting petrol, you name it. It was completely understandable. Maeve's beauty was captivating and her personality infectious. She was magnifying, with perfectly dense midnight black curls and deep caramel skin that looked like silk, an hourglass figure and freckles kissing her nose—the sort of beauty that one could only dream of having, especially in a town like this.

Maeve stood out from day one. She was one of the only bi-racial people in our town and the only one in our year at school. It was a small rural town with no culture other than its own.

Maeve had always been treated differently.

When we were younger, she was teased for being different. She pretended it hadn't bothered her—even though it had—but she would always stand up for herself.

When Maeve went through puberty, she went from being teased to being adored. Our peers had finally realised how beautiful she was, and everyone became desperate for her attention.

She hadn't just stood up for herself growing up. She had always stood up for me. She was my protector. Outspoken, brash and confident (all the things I wasn't) but she was gentler and kinder when it came to me, especially since Mum had died and my… *issues* had begun. She was the only one who knew.

"He's bringing a friend," she added cautiously. "*Brilliant.* Can't wait." I rolled my eyes.

"Oh stop! I like this one. I promise it will be the last time I make you do this, please." she wallowed dramatically.

"Okay, okay," I laughed.

"I don't know if you remember him, but he's so hot and sweet." Her pupils widened as she spoke about him.

I knew of Alex. He was two years above us, so we had always been on a different campus, but we would see him around town or on nights out. There were only three pubs here, so it was hard to escape anyone. He was about six foot four and a bit dopey looking, but he always seemed nice enough, especially compared to the rest of the guys in this town.

"Didn't you just call him lanky?" I raised an eyebrow.

Maeve kicked me under the table as she looked over my head. "Shush, he's here." She began fixing her hair.

I sighed. Another night of sitting through painfully awkward small talk with a guy who has no interest in me, and who I have no interest in either. It was always obvious from the moment they sat next to me that they were disappointed they were going to have to entertain me for the night. A handful would get too drunk and attempt to sleep with me, which led to me trying to sneak off home without them noticing. I couldn't think of anything worse than losing my virginity to one of them.

Maeve stood up from the table and smiled her wide toothy smile, her arms open as she went to embrace him.

"Hey Maeve, you look lovely," Alex said sweetly as he grabbed her waist and kissed her on the cheek.

"Thanks, babe." She tried hiding her grin. "You know Lou,

right?" She gestured towards me.

Alex turned to me and held out his hand. "Of course. Hi Lou." I had to admit, he was a lot fitter than I remembered. "My friend, Zack, is here too. He's just getting us some drinks. Do you guys want anything?"

"Two more glasses of rosé for us, please." Maeve looked adoringly up at him as she replied.

Alex turned away and walked towards the bar.

"Maeve, do you like him?" I was flummoxed. I had never seen her this giddy before.

"Oh, shut up! He's just a sweetheart, isn't he?" She reached round to catch a glimpse of him at the bar. "And look at him. He's beautiful." She paused and turned back towards me. "I recognise his friend, but I can't place where I would've seen him." I could see her looking someone up and down. "He's very good looking, though."

I didn't turn around. There was no point. He wouldn't be interested in me anyway.

Maeve smiled as Alex re-joined the table with the bottle of wine, taking the seat next to her. The chair next to me was pulled out from under the table.

"Hi. Louise, right? I'm Zack." His voice was like butter, smooth and deep. I didn't know if he was just being polite, but he sounded genuinely pleased to meet me.

I turned to see the face behind the voice. His eyes were the first thing I noticed. They were the sort of blue you could get lost in, looking at all the different flecks of colour. They stood out even more against his brown wavy hair and olive skin. He smiled at me, his soft pink lips lifting at the corners to expose his perfectly straight teeth, his eyes wrinkled in the corners as he smiled.

My heart skipped a beat, I had never had a feeling like this before, starting in my toes to my heart up to my head, like a rush of adrenaline; his smile was like a drug.

A shot of pain took over my shin a kick under the table pulled me out of my frozen state. I turned as Maeve was looking at me wide-eyed.

"Erm. Hi. Yeah, call me Lou," I looked back at Maeve awkwardly, trying not to make eye contact with him.

He sat down next to me, placing two beers on the table for him and Alex. I smiled sheepishly. As soon as he sat next to me, I felt his overwhelming presence in my whole body, invading my personal space.

"Guess those two are in for a good night," he laughed, nodding towards Maeve and Alex.

I looked back at them to see their tongues down each other's throats, oblivious to the fact they had company.

Awkwardly I gazed up at Zack through my eyelashes and half smiled, unable to think of anything intelligent to say. I could barely form a sentence with him next to me. His arm was so close to mine as the table was too small for four, and we were crowded together.

I could feel the electricity radiating from his body.

"Zack just moved back here with his Mum," Alex said when

he finally came up for air.

"Oh cool. Where did you live before?" questioned Maeve.

"I lived here till I was fourteen, then when my parents split, Mum and I moved to York. My grandma isn't very well, so we have come back to look after her." Zack's eyes lowered awkwardly as if he regretted sharing so much. He reached for his drink, exposing the inside of his forearm.

I noticed a tattoo sprawled across the length of it, a traditional style tattoo of a fortune teller. She had long black hair that was adorned with a purple shawl. I had never seen a tattoo with such detail before.

"I just got it. I drew it myself." I looked up to see him watching me eye it up.

"Wow. You drew that?" I exhaled. "It's beautiful."

"Yeah. I'm starting a tattoo apprenticeship soon," he added. "Do you have any?"

"Not yet. I would like some though," I looked at him thoughtfully.

"Maybe I could tattoo you one day." He smiled, and my heart skipped a beat.

I spent the night too engrossed in Zack's words to speak my own. He spoke of his favourite art, books and films and told us when he began to draw for the first time. There were so many layers to him, more than just football and beer like every other man I had encountered. I had never met anyone like him.

Alex began whispering in Maeve's ear. She started

giggling, and I knew exactly what was coming. They had been all over each other all night. I was surprised they had entertained us for as long as they had.

"I think we are going to head off," Alex predictably announced.

Maeve looked at me, mouthing 'sorry', her eyes pleading with me. I smiled at her, giving her my unspoken permission. I could tell she liked Alex, and I didn't want to get in the way of that, no matter how much I didn't want the night to end.

"I could walk you home if you like, Lou?"

I turned my head abruptly, my eyes widened as Zack smiled at me gently. "You don't have to. It's not far," I said.

"No, I want to." His eyes twinkled in the light. "We can talk about all the tattoos I'm going to give you." He nudged me playfully.

I looked at Maeve for reassurance, but she just looked at me encouragingly.

"That's very kind of you, Zack. I would feel much better knowing Lou won't be walking home
alone in the dark." She smiled sweetly, knowing full well I was fine on my own. "We should all get together again soon."

"Yeah, definitely." Zack smirked.

We all headed towards the door and into the outside car park to say goodbye.

Maeve pulled me in for a tight hug. "You're welcome," she whispered into my ear.

"You owe me," I whispered back through gritted teeth.

She kissed me on the cheek before letting me go. "Bye, I'll call you tomorrow, Lou." She grabbed Alex's hand, walking in the opposite direction.

Zack and I stood still for a moment, unsure of what to say now that we were alone. The air was heavy with tension, and I wasn't sure if it was just me who was feeling it.

"So, shall we go?" He gestured for me to start walking.

I nodded and made my way across the road. It was cooler now the sun had long since set. I crossed my arms over my body, rubbing my hands against them to get some warmth.

"Here." Zack began removing his hoodie.

"Oh no, it's fine, don't worry," I rushed.

"No, take it. I insist." He handed his hoodie out to me.

"Thank you," I murmured, it smelt like washing powder and cigarettes.

"So, what's your story?" he said. "You seem like someone with a story."

"What makes you say that?" I pulled my hair over my face, suddenly feeling as though a spotlight had been cast over me.

"Your eyes. Your eyes look like they're full of unsaid things." He looked at me with a mixture of humour and seriousness on his face.

"Well, I've lived here my whole life with my little sister, Faye, and my Dad—but I'm going to leave here one day to be a writer." I didn't know what had come over me, I was normally very guarded.

"Where's your mum?"

I paused, inhaling a sharp breath. "She died four years ago. Cancer."

"That's awful. I'm sorry. I don't know what I would do without my mum."

I looked up at him, noticing his height compared to mine, tall and strong. His eyes were filled with a deep pain.

"I don't have anything to do with my Dad, though, he's a horrible man, so it's okay." I could tell he was sharing his issues to level the playing field.

"Why?" I asked.

He shuffled uncomfortably, "He used to knock Mum around. Me too, once I was old enough." He was looking into the distance as if the memories were flickering through his mind. "One night, she caught him cheating on her with a woman from around the corner. When she confronted him, he threw her down the stairs and broke her ribs." He bit his lip, holding back his emotion. But I could see the anger building on his face as he spoke. "So, she packed our stuff when he was at work one day and moved us as far away as she could."

"Is she not scared she'll see him again being back here?" I couldn't stop thinking about how terrified they both must be, being so close to him again.

"He's in prison now. He got done for doing the same to his second wife." His brows furrowed. "Guess she had the balls to press charges." I sensed annoyance in his voice. He shrugged, dismissing the conversation.

We continued to walk in the cool breeze, both silent. I was paranoid I had pushed it too far with my questioning, yet I was desperate for the conversation to continue.

"I've got an idea for a book," I blurted out.

He stopped in his tracks, his eyes lighting up. "Oh yeah?" He smiled. "Tell me everything."

I kept walking. "It's about this kingdom, in another world. There are two rival soldiers. They meet during the war for the throne and fall in love, despite it being a crime punishable by death."

He quickened his walk, catching up with me. "Well, Louise, I think it's imperative that you write that book because it sounds amazing." His smile was bright. "I want to be the first to read it."

"One day," I mused.

"Why not now? You're done with school, right?"

"I just don't know if Dad would be able to cope without me," I admitted.

"I'm sure your Dad will be okay. Surely, he wouldn't want you to put your life on hold for him?" I knew he was right. Dad would want me to go. It was more my own fears holding me back.

I sighed. "Probably."

We'd approached the estate, my house appeared in the foreground as we rounded the corner. The streetlights shone on his face. I could finally make out all of his features. His jaw was strong and sprinkled with stubble; his skin dotted with freckles.

"This is me," I said, gesturing towards my house. I continued until we were at the end of the drive, stopping far enough away so that no one in the house would hear us. A family interrogation about a boy dropping me home was the last thing I needed.

I unzipped the hoodie and slipped it off my arms, handing it back to him. "Thank you."

He took the hoodie from my hands, not saying a word. He was looking at me, really looking at me. I felt bare, naked, my soul on full display… yet I felt safe sharing that with him. I had never felt this seen by anyone, and I didn't want it to stop. His eyes twinkled as he studied my face. He began to open his mouth as if he had something he wanted to say, but instead, he closed his mouth and took a deep breath.

"Bye Lou, it was nice to meet you." He smiled at me sheepishly and began walking away. Once he was a few meters from me, he turned to look back at me. He didn't say anything. He didn't smile. He just stood there taking me in before calling over to me. "Write that book, Lou." He stared at me a moment longer before turning and walking into the night.

I opened the front door and made my way inside, smiling from ear to ear. My breath was fast as I entered the dark house. Elation encompassed me, like something in me had changed all from this chance encounter. I had only known him for a few hours, but it felt like I had known him all my life.

The light from my bedroom shone into the landing as I

tiptoed up the stairs. Closing the door behind me, I grabbed the laptop from my desk and sat on my bed. I lifted the screen and opened a blank document and began typing.

Chapter 1.

Louise Present Day

And in the blink of an eye, I was eighteen again.

I felt like I couldn't breathe. My chest was tight, like someone was sitting on top of me.

I breathed in deep, trying to get as much air to my lungs as possible, bracing myself knowing that my heart was about to break all over again.

No matter the time or distance, every time I saw him, I was back to square one, simultaneously falling in love and falling to pieces. I turned around slowly, trying not to tremble.

His eyes twinkled at me, and his hair was shorter, a small beard had grown with splashes of ginger running through it. He'd aged slightly, the wrinkles in the corners of his eyes were deeper but he still took my breath away, even now.

He was wearing an open black cord shirt with a white t-shirt underneath, which perfectly showed off his slight muscles.

"Hi," I said breathlessly.

"Hey." He stood, taking me in. "Lou, you look…" He stopped as if he hadn't finished whatever he was about to say. He cleared his throat, eyeing me for a moment, before asking, "how have you been?"

It was the normal thing to say, but the question was loaded with hidden meaning.

It had been two years since I had last seen him, I was in the darkest place of my life, but now wasn't the time to go into that.

"I'm good. How are you?"

"Great, yeah. I'm just here with some guys from work. I take it you still live here?" I could sense the concern in his voice—concern for what, I didn't know. Maybe that I still harboured a lot of hatred for him? I winced, thinking back to the last conversion we'd had.

"Yeah," I reeled back to his earlier statement. "Wait. Do you live here now?" The last time wehad seen each other, he was living with his girlfriend, Grace, back home.

He nodded. "Moved here about a year ago."

My heart sank. He'd moved here and never reached out.

"Look, I need to get back to them," he said, gesturing to his table, chewing the inside of his lip. "I would love to see you again and catch up properly, if you wouldn't mind. But, uh, it's totally fine if you do. I was just thinking, do you maybe want to go for a drink this weekend?" His eyes were full of hope. "I understand if you don't want to.".

I mulled it over, pausing for a moment. I knew it was a bad idea to let him into my life again but seeing him standing right in front of me felt like fate was screaming at us.

My heart replied before my head could intervene. "I'd like that."

His eyes lit up, his lips twitching into a smile. "Great. Is your number the same?"

"Yeah, same number."

"Cool. I'll text you later. Have a good night."

"Yeah, you too," I muttered, still in shock. What the hell was going on?

Zack looked at me once more, a thousand unsaid words on his lips. "It is great to see you, Lou."

I nodded and watched as he walked away.

Turning back towards the bar, I held onto it, stopping myself from falling. My heart was racing. I could feel my skin getting warmer, my breath quick, and a lump forming in my throat. My body felt like I had been shot several times straight through the heart.

"Are you okay?" I looked up to see the bartender looking at me, concerned.

"Yes, thank you. Can I get some water, please?" I smiled at him gently, hoping he wouldn't press further.

Shrugging, he pulled a glass from the side, filling it under the tap. I took my water and headed back outside towards Kayleigh.

"I got his number," she elated as I approached the table.

She looked at me as I sat down. "You good?"

I didn't want to tell her the truth, she knew all about Zack, and I just needed to process it before telling her.

"Yeah. I think I should go home, too much champagne," I lied, forcing a weak laugh.

She looked me up and down unsure "Okay, babe. Get home and have a good night's sleep." She nodded towards the waiter, "I've got dessert for later."

I stood up and grabbed my bag, reaching over to hug Kayleigh. "Eat him alive," I teased. Waving goodbye, I began walking slowly back home, grateful that the air had slightly cooled off. I was still sweating from my encounter without the added humidity from earlier that day.

When I entered my apartment, it felt different from when I left just a few hours previous. It was heavy somehow; lonely and dark.

Heading to the bathroom, I turned the shower on, moving the tap to cold. My body became very aware of my clothes clinging to my body. My breath was getting quicker, and my skin was burning as the anxiety rose through me.

I pulled my clothes off forcefully, desperate to get them off and stepped into the shower and sat down on the cold ceramic, letting the cold water pour over me. I looked down at my wrist, tracing the outline of the sunflower that was tattooed onto my skin.

I tried to rationalise what had happened. Seeing him again didn't have to mean anything; we had been through so much together that maybe we could finally just be friends. I was a different person now; stronger, happier. Maybe we could be in each other's lives without all the pain this time.

Once I felt somewhat myself again, I stood and turned the water off, stepping out of the shower, leaving a puddle on the bathmat as I reached for my dressing gown. I turned off the light and walked along the hall to my bedroom, crawling straight into my bed, pulling the duvet up to my ears.

I was ready for this day to end. Closing my eyes, I had let myself drift off when my phone vibrated from my bedside table, disrupting my slumber.

I reached over, knowing it was probably Kayleigh checking that I had got home safe. I looked at my phone and saw a message from an unknown number. My stomach spasmed. It was him.

Hey Lou. Sorry we couldn't talk much. I meant what I said though, it was great to see you. Are you free tomorrow night for a drink? Zack.

I knew he said he'd text me tonight, but I hadn't expected him to message so soon. I stared at the message for a few minutes, reading the words over and over again, mulling over what to reply.

Hey, sounds good. Let me know when and where. It

was good to see you too.

I put my phone on silent and placed it back on the table, rolling over. I closed my eyes and let the exhaustion take over. The day had been so momentous with finishing the book and seeing Zack. I was emotionally and physically drained. I fell asleep that night quicker than I had in a long time.

*

It was a hot day, one of those scolding August days that England gets once in a while, the sort of heat that made it unbearable to do anything. I was meeting Zack that evening at a local tapas bar.

I'd spent the day fighting the heat whilst trying to catch up on the things I had been neglecting cleaning the flat, washing piles of clothes, changing the bedding and paying bills.

Kayleigh texted, interrupting my productivity.

Hope you're feeling better. Let me know if you need anything. My night was WILD.

I laughed at her message. At least I didn't ruin the rest of her night.

Much better, thank you. Glad you had fun! Can't wait to hear all about it.

Today, I felt confident. Ready to meet my past head on. I was wearing a strappy top tied up to just show a hint of my midriff, paired with a black flowery midi skirt and Dr. Martens. The perfect mix of casual nonchalance and 'how good do I look'. My hair was even cooperating, and my waves were effortless and tame, instead of their usual frizz.

I walked out of my building feeling the butterflies swarming around inside my stomach.

I remembered that I was once told that butterflies were your body's way of warning you of incoming danger. There was more riding on tonight than just reconciliation. I needed to prove that I could be around him without falling apart.

I let my mind explore the possibilities of how the night might play out.

Would he want to talk about that day when everything fell apart? I hoped not. Was he still with Grace? I also hoped not.

It was busy when I got to the bar, groups of friends crowding the outside tables, a cloud of cigarette smoke surrounding them. I walked inside the restaurant, letting my eyes adjust to the sea of wood planters and greenery adorning the walls, so busy it was making it hard to focus on anything.

I was hoping I was the first one here, so I could have a minute to compose myself. I looked around to see if I could spot him amongst the tables, but the room was too large and bright to find him.

"Welcome. Do you have a reservation?" A server interrupted my gaze.

"Hi. Yes. Maybe under Zack or, uh, Taylor?" I stuttered, still trying to look around to see if I could spot him.

"Perfect, the other member of the party is already seated. Follow me."

I groaned quietly, knowing I wouldn't have any time to prepare.

I followed the waitress through the restaurant and down a flight of stairs, which led to more seating. It was just as garish as upstairs.

She escorted me right to the back of the restaurant to a booth in the corner.

There he was. He looked up at me brightly, his contagious smile melting me already. He stood up to greet me, but I sat down quickly before he could hug me.

I knew I needed to keep him at arm's length to keep a straight head.

He seemed somewhat put out by my abrupt greeting as he sat back down. "I ordered you a glass of pinot. I hope that's still okay."

"Thanks," I said, hiding my frustration that he still knew my order.

"You look nice." He cleared his throat.

I bit my lip. He looked good too, not that I would admit that aloud. He was wearing a navy blue shirt that made his eyes pop. His tattoos were visible where his sleeves had been rolled up. I spotted the fortune-teller's mouth peeping out. She was now surrounded by many other tattoos, including a bright red rose.

I could smell his cologne across the table, the nostalgia of it making my stomach feel uneasy.

"You too, you look so...old." My eyes widened, realising how rude that had sounded. Even for a writer, I didn't have a way with words.

He almost spat out his drink, holding back a laugh. "Well, that's what happens when you're approaching thirty."

"Sorry, I didn't mean that. I just mean older."

winced. "How's the tattooing going?"

"Good, actually, that's the reason I moved here, to open up my own studio."

"Did you? That's amazing! You must be so happy." I couldn't hide my genuine smile.

His body relaxed. "You always believed in me, Lou. I just needed to believe in myself… Well, that and get some cash." He laughed. "I saved all my money, sold the house and took the plunge."

"You sold the house?"

"Yeah. Grace and I broke up for good, and it just didn't feel like home anymore—for either of us. So, I decided to move to London. There was nothing left for me back home."

I kept my face still, not wanting him to see my relief. "I'm sorry, that must have been hard."

He shrugged. "She deserved better. I didn't treat her right."

He didn't need to carry on. We both knew what he had done. As much as I hadn't liked her, she didn't deserve what had happened.

"Alex is here, and well, I guess you are, too."

My heart stopped. I was here, I'd always been here. "Oh," I managed. "Well, I'm sure Alex likes having
you around."

He grimaced, but he didn't explain himself, he just changed the subject. "What about you? Is there another book coming?"

"Well, actually, when you saw me last night, I was out celebrating finishing it."

He looked at me with wide eyes. "Wow. Can I get the first copy? I am your number one fan, you know.

I rolled my eyes at him. I had always wondered if he'd read the first book. Without him giving me that push, there probably would never have been a book to begin with.

"I'll see what I can do," I teased.

"Thank you." He smirked. "So, are you with anyone at the moment?"

"No," I said, wiping the condensation off my glass. "I haven't… since Chris," I whispered, pausing for a moment before adding, "What about you?"

"No, nothing serious since Grace."

I exhaled. I was relieved he was no longer with her. I
never thought she was good enough for him.

But right now, I was scared. We hadn't both been single at the same time for almost a decade.

I nodded and raised my glass. "Well, cheers to being single… and to failed relationships'

He nodded back with a polite smile as our glasses clinked together.

The room suddenly became heavy with the words we had never said, heavy with the words we wanted to say but never would, never could.

The evening continued; the conversation flowed as did the drinks. We quickly fell back into our old ways, the awkwardness dissipating.

We caught each other up on the last few years of our lives, avoiding mentioning our past as much as we could. I knew we were kidding ourselves, pretending that our history hadn't existed. But being here, together, it all had fallen away. It was like there was no one else in the room, in the world, but us.

"Guess we should get going before we get kicked out." I looked around to see the restaurant was empty, the waitresses cleaning down the empty tables, looking at us expectantly.

It felt like we had only been here an hour. I looked at my watch; it was close to midnight.

We stood up from the table, Zack throwing down a few notes from his wallet, and walked back up the stairs and out into the street.

"Fancy a walk?" Zack asked, eyeing me.

My heart skipped a beat. “Sure,” I replied far too quickly. I hated to admit it to myself, but I wasn’t ready for the night to be over.

We walked side by side, the electricity between us palpable.

“Lou, I know you probably don’t want to talk about this,” he began.

I gulped. I knew what was coming.

“What happened the last time we saw each other, I am so sorry. It was all my fault.”

“No.” I sighed. “We were both to blame.” What happened that day shouldn’t have happened, we had both been in a bad place, especially me, but I couldn’t let him take all the blame.

“I feel like I took advantage of you.”

I turned to look at him. “I know that I was a mess, but I couldn’t have gotten through that day without you. I’m sorry people got hurt, but I am not sorry it happened.”

He caught my eye as he exhaled deeply. He looked relieved, like a weight had been lifted.

We continued walking, both trying to think of a new topic. That had been enough of the history of us for one night.

“So, what’s the new book about?”

“Well, Evelyn and Tarlin have to find their way back to each other after they got separated during the War for the Midnight Throne.” I paused, testing to see if he had actually read my first book.

“How do they manage that when the Grand Trine is now

watching over the realm?"

I smiled, impressed. "I'm not giving anything else away."

"Is there anything I can do to get answers out of you?" He smirked.

"Sorry." I raised my brows at him, teasing him. "Anyway, enough about me, tell me about the shop."

"It's great, honestly, I love the place," he began. "I walked past it one day when the owner was there - it was a rundown clothing shop and the landlord was struggling to find new tenants, and I just thought it would be perfect for a tattoo studio. I'd love to show you it,"

"I'd like that."

"Maybe, I could tattoo you again soon?" his voice sounded jokey as we approached the corner of my street.

"Maybe." I wasn't sure I needed another daily reminder of him on my body.

We slowed down as we approached the door to my flat. The tension between us grew, knowing it was almost time to say goodbye. We stopped and faced each other, he looked at me in that way he always had.

"Thank you for tonight, Lou." He smiled softly. "My life's not been as bright since you haven't been in it." I felt his arms wrap around my waist as he pulled me close to him. I could feel the energy move between our bodies. "I've missed you," he whispered so quietly I almost couldn't hear, his face buried in my hair.

I pulled away, gently pushing him back. I knew I needed

to tread carefully. If I had let him hold me just a moment longer, I wasn't sure I would ever let go.

Was I really going to let him back into my life this easily after everything we had been through?

"Bye, Zack." I pulled away and stepped back.

"Bye, Lou."

I felt his eyes watching me as I made my way into my flat. I couldn't keep the smile off my face despite my head knowing what a bad idea this was. My heart couldn't help it.

Maybe it could be different this time.

Louise 2012

A week had passed since Zack, and I had met. My days were busy, working in a local restaurant, as well as writing my book with my newfound creativity. But even with all that going on, I still hadn't been able to get him off my mind.

Maeve rang me the next morning, after Zack walked me home. I played it cool, told her I thought he was nice enough and hadn't thought much else.

She wasn't convinced. She knew me too well. But thankfully, she didn't probe me again.

My book was in full swing. I had written the first eight chapters in the last week. My brain was on fire, creating faraway worlds, unexpected heroes, ancient wars and forbidden love.

It was a Friday afternoon, and I was on the lunch shift at work. A few old people were enjoying their early bird dinner.

I scrolled absentmindedly through my phone, hiding behind the bar so no one could see me avoiding my actual work.

A message from Maeve popped up at the top of my phone.

Do you want to go for some drinks in the city tonight with Alex and me?

I hadn't seen her for a few days; she had been consumed in her Alex bubble, and I had been distracted consumed by my own writing one.

Part of me wanted to say no and just go home to keep writing, but I knew I couldn't stay locked up.

Maeve was off to uni in a few weeks, and I needed to see her as much as possible before she left. I had seen her almost every day for the last eighteen years, and I knew that once she left,

I would miss her more than anything.

I was going to be living at home still. Hopefully uni would keep me distracted, and maybe I'd even meet some new friends.

I looked back at my phone and began typing.

I'd love to. X

*

The bus arrived in the city in the early evening. The bar we had arranged to meet at was only a few streets away. It was part cocktail bar, part crazy golf, and it sounded like hell to an athletically challenged individual such as myself.

I hovered outside the bar, leaning against the wall, not wanting to go in on my own. I began scrolling through the list of books I still needed to buy for my university course.

Suddenly, I felt a tap on my shoulder, pulling me out of my head.

I jumped, almost dropping my phone.

"Sorry, I didn't mean to scare you." It was Zack, his voice was penetrating, his touch lingered where it had been on my shoulder. "Are you okay?"

He was wearing a long-sleeved top under a Ramones t-shirt, paired with skinny jeans. He looked perfect.

"Oh, hey, what are you doing here? Are you meeting Alex and Maeve?" It was typical of Maeve to play secret matchmaker. She hadn't mentioned Zack was coming.

"Yeah, did they not tell you? I hope you don't mind me crashing."

I relaxed my face and smiled at him. "Not at all."

"Come on, let's go get some drinks whilst we wait. Need to calm your nerves after the fright I just gave you." He smirked, pulled the door of the bar open, and placed his hand on the small of my back, leading me through the crowd ahead of him. His touch turned me to jelly. "What would you like?"

"Whatever you're having," I smiled, trying not to be awkward.

"Two Pornstars, and a large nachos please," he asked the waitress. I couldn't help but giggle. "What's so funny?" He looked at me, amused.

"I just didn't take you for a cocktail guy."

"You shouldn't judge a book by its cover, Lou. You of all people should know that." He smiled at me. My heart fluttered at the way my name sounded out of his mouth.

"That'll be fourteen quid, mate." The bartender handed Zack the drinks.

The room was surrounded with couples, laughing and joking round the course. I became very aware suddenly about what we must look like sat together. They probably wondered how a girl like me got a guy like him.

Zack looked at me, then around the room. It was loud, too loud to talk. He reached down and grabbed the leg of my stool, pulling my full weight towards him.

"I want to be able to hear you." He smiled, not taking his eyes off me. "Have some of these." He pushed the plate of nachos towards me, and I obliged, covering my mouth as I ate.

"I started my book," I blurted out, needing to say something to stop me from melting under his gaze.

"Have you really? Lou, that's amazing. When can I read it?"

"Never," I half-joked.

"No! I honestly can't wait to read it. Just remember me when you're famous."

"You don't need to worry about that. Anyway, did you hear

anything back about the apprenticeship?"

"Well, funny you should ask. I signed the contract yesterday. It starts in a month; they've asked me to
prepare some sketches." His eyes lit up; I could tell how much he wanted it.

"That's amazing. Have you got any ideas?"

"Let's just say, I'm feeling inspired. I'll show you my sketches. I'd like your opinion on them, anyway."

"I don't know anything about art." My cheeks prickled with heat, not sure why my opinion would matter.

"That's okay. I want to know what you think." He pushed my leg playfully.

I smiled. I didn't know what to reply. I didn't know how to flirt back. *Was he even flirting?* I had no idea.

Of course, he wasn't flirting with me. Someone like him could *never* like someone like me.

I wasn't good enough for him. I wasn't good enough for anyone. Here I was stuffing my face with food like the pig I was.

I could feel the heat rising in my chest. I tried to shake it off, but the thoughts were too strong.

"I just need to go to the toilet quickly." I got up and rushed away before I could hear his response.

I pushed open the bathroom door and ran into a cubicle, frantically locking the door behind me. I slammed up the toilet seat and forced my fingers deep into the back of my throat
uncomfortable as the sharp edges of the nachos poked at my throat.

Beads of sweat formed on the top of my forehead as the sick raced into my mouth.

The automatic release cascaded over me, like the bad thoughts were leaving my body as I purged.

I pulled away from the toilet, panting and walked back into the bathroom and took a look in the mirror. My eyes were bloodshot, my nose running, and the reality of what I was doing was staring back at me.

The high never lasted long.

I took a mint out of my bag, fixed my eyeliner and regained my composure before I walked back into the bar.

As I came around the corner, back into the bar area, Maeve and Alex were standing at the table with Zack.

"Hey," I greeted them, trying to act casual.

Maeve looked me up and down, concerned, her brow furrowed, and her eyes narrowed.

"Hi, Lou." She said slowly, she raised her brows at me as if to ask 'are you okay?' I gave her a quick nod and smile to reassure her.

Maeve clocked on to what was going on about six months ago, she had confronted me then and there, and it was the only fight we had ever had. We didn't speak for a week. She had been supporting me ever since, always being someone to cry to or talk to. At first, I resisted her help but now it was my only solace when things got too much.

"Hey Lou, hope Zack's been keeping you entertained,"

Alex laughed at Zack.

Zack shot him a disapproving look. “We’ve had a great chat. Haven’t we, Lou?” Zack turned his head to me, looking for backup.

"Yeah, he’s kept me entertained, don’t worry.” I smiled.

We made our way through to the desk and collected our golf clubs; it felt like a double date, but I talked myself down before the bad thoughts ran through my head again.

We worked our way around the course, laughing as Maeve missed almost every shot and Zack got overly competitive with Alex. I was surprised by how well I did. I even got a hole in one, and Zack put his arm around me when I had, causing me to almost have a heart attack there and then.

We’d had so much fun that we decided to play another round, ordering more cocktails as we made our way around again.

Maeve was the star of the show, laughing a little too loud and screaming with glee when she hit the ball into the hole. Alex, of course, watched her every move with puppy eyes.

They complimented each other perfectly. I was so happy she’d found someone who loved her as much as I did.

The night drew to a close, and we huddled out the bar in stitches of laughter.

“Well, I’m glad we know who the winner is, once and for all.” Zack teased, raising his hands above his head in victory.

“Only because the rest of us are tipsy. If I was drinking water all night I would have won too.” Alex protested.

“Keep telling yourself that mate.” Zack pushed him in the

arm.

"Did you get the bus, Lou? Mum is picking us up. We can take you back," Maeve suggested.

"That would be great." I didn't fancy sitting on the bus for another hour.

"It's okay. I'll take her back, gives me some company on the drive home," Zack interrupted.

"Are you sure?" I asked.

"What an excellent idea, Zack," Maeve's smile was nothing but smug.

"Erm, okay, thanks," I smiled trying to hide my awkwardness.

We said our goodbyes and began walking to the car park down the road from the bar.

"Sorry about the mess," he said, opening the car door for me.

"Thanks," I muttered, looking around, confused. There was no mess to speak of.

Zack drove one-handed out of the car park, his sharp jawline even more prominent from the side. The lump returned in my throat as the tension mounted between us, filling the car, causing a tightness to build through my body.

I reached for the button and rolled down the window, attempting to get as much fresh air into my lungs as possible.

"I like the two of them together. I've never seen Alex with a girlfriend before," Zack said, interrupting the silence.

"Same. Maeve never really seems that interested in any of the guys she dates." I paused, realising that probably didn't paint Maeve in the best light. "Not that she dates loads of guys," I added. "I really hope they last when she goes to Leeds."

"I forgot about her going to uni. What are you doing next year?" He looked over at me. There was something in his eyes that I couldn't quite read.

"Staying here. I'm going to Nottingham Trent to do creative writing."

"Because of your Dad and sister?"

"I guess, yeah." That was the only reason I was staying local, but I didn't want to fully admit that to myself, let alone him.

"Where would you have gone if they weren't in the picture?" he probed.

"London," I answered immediately.

"If you don't mind me asking, why do they need you at home?"

I sighed. "I guess they don't, really. I just worry about my dad he's been on his own since my Mum and I don't want him to get lonely or not take care of himself."

"You should go. I know you're worried, but you have to do what's best for you. Don't you think he could manage?"

He was probably right, Dad was more than capable of standing on his own two feet. It was me who was scared to leave him. We hadn't left each other since Mum died, no more than a night away here and there.

"Yeah, he could, I'm not sure if I'm ready, to be honest,"

He looked at me, his eyes warm and reassuring. "The scariest place you can be is in the comfort zone."

I laughed out loud. "Where did you read that?" "My mum has a canvas of it in the kitchen," he said before bursting into laughter. It was the most beautiful sound I'd ever heard.

"Will you move into the city when you start the apprenticeship?" I asked, getting the topic off
me.

"I'll stay at home for a bit to save money, and then get a flat, probably. I've been working in a clothes shop since I left school as a start—and to help mum out—but she knew how much I wanted this, so she told me to go for it."

"Your mum sounds great."

"She is. She's so supportive and strong; she's never let what happened with my Dad get in her way."

His face lit up just talking about her. "She's a lot
like you, putting her family first all the time." He kept his eyes on the road as he spoke. "Well, if you do stay, at least we can keep each other company."

The car was quiet for a moment.

"Can I ask you something personal? Please don't get upset?"

I was confused about what he could possibly ask that would upset me. "Erm, okay?"

"Did I upset you earlier?"

“What do you mean?”

“When you went to the toilet, your eyes were really red after, and I wasn’t sure if you’d been crying.”

My heart sank into my stomach, and my mouth went dry. “No, I wasn’t crying.”

“Oh, sorry. You just looked upset. I just wanted to check everything’s okay. I thought it was me.”

“No, it wasn’t. I was sick,” I blurted out, my eyes pricked unsure why I had just divulged that.

“Oh. Are you not feeling well?”

“No... I am fine. It’s fine.” I stuttered. My brain was working overtime and the I could feel the colour draining from my face. I kept my head forward staring at the road flash by but I could feel his eyes on me.

“Oh, erm sorry, you don’t have to talk about it. It's none of my business.” I didn’t know what he was thinking but I needed this conversation to end.

“I don’t want to talk about it,” I whispered.

“Okay. . . I’m sorry.” he sounded deflated.

“No. . . I am fine. It’s fine.” I stuttered. My brain was working overtime and the I could feel the colour draining from my face. I kept my head forward staring at the road flash by but I could feel his eyes on me.

“Oh, erm sorry, you don’t have to talk about it. It's none of my business.” I didn’t know what he was thinking but I needed this conversation to end.

"I don't want to talk about it," I whispered.

"Okay. . . I'm sorry. he sounded deflated, beaten.

We sat in silence for what felt like an eternity. I knew I needed to explain myself so he didn't think I was some fucked up mess.

"I make myself sick. It's just a release," I began. He looked at me, surprised that I was answering him. "I eat and then I make myself sick. Eating makes me feel like I'm spiralling, and this helps. Anytime I'm upset or don't feel good enough, it releases it. It doesn't last long, but the temporary control it gives me calms me down I guess," I explained.

"Why wouldn't you be good enough?" He looked at me, his brows furrowed when I didn't reply. "How long have you been doing it for?"

"It started when Mum died. Well, my therapist reckons I felt guilty I couldn't save her or that God was punishing me for not being good enough, and that meant I didn't deserve to keep my Mum, pathetic, huh?" I took a deep breath. It did sound pathetic, especially saying it out loud.

He stayed silent. My leg began to tap nervously, scared I had exposed too much of myself.

I looked out the window as we approached my street. He drove up to the house and stopped the car, pulling his handbrake up. He turned towards me in his seat, looking at me up and down.

Our eyes locked. There was no sympathy or pity in his eyes; he was just seeing me for who I was; the good, the bad and the ugly.

He reached over and grabbed my hand, and my breathing became heavy. “You are good enough. You are more than good enough, Lou.” He lent in, and I felt the soft pressure from his lips brush my cheek.

My heart stopped. And as he backed away, I felt the prickle of his kiss linger on my skin.

“Night, Lou,”

“Night, Zack.”

Louise Present Day

“So, I sent the final draft off to the publishers, and we just need to sign off on the cover at the meeting next week and then it’s pretty much a go,” Kayleigh explained.

“And in terms of marketing?” I asked, jotting everything down in my planner.

“Just continue to interact with readers on your socials as much as possible. The team will sort the big stuff. We’ve got plenty of time, and you’ve got a lot of loyal fans waiting for the next book, so pre-sales should be good.”

“Okay, I’ll keep making content and replying to readers.”

“Yes, great.” Kayleigh finished typing and closed her laptop. “That’s enough business for one day. So, what’s going on with you?”

“What do you mean?” I wasn’t sure if she had suspected something or was just making conversation.

Kayleigh looked me up and down questionably. "Lou, don't lie. Who's the guy?" She prodded me in the leg.

I sighed. I should have known better than to try and hide anything from her. "Not a guy. *The guy*."

"Oh, shit." Kayleigh stood up from my couch and headed for the kitchen, opening the fridge door. Luckily, the only thing I ever really had in there was wine and a bottle of vodka that I kept for emergencies.

Kayleigh came back with both.

I laughed. "I think just the wine for now."

She sighed, looking at me sideways with a recognisable note of disapproval, and poured the wine into two glasses, handing me one. "Okay. Explain."

"He was at the bar on Friday, and we bumped into each other." I tried to sound as collected as possible.

Her eyes widened. "And?"

"And, then we met up for a drink the next day."

"Oh my god, Louise! Did you have sex with him?" "No!" I exclaimed. "There is way too much… stuff between us for a one-night stand, and I'm not even sure he sees me that way anymore. I can't believe you think I would!"

"You can't blame me, I couldn't be sure with all your history. And don't be ridiculous, Lou, of course he sees you that way. So, what happened then if you didn't sleep together?"

"We just... chatted." It was hard to explain when I didn't know myself. "He's single now, though."

She raised her eyebrows "Mmhmm."

"But we are just friends."

"Mmhmm." She raised her eyebrows even higher. "Look, Lou, I know there is a lot of history between you guys, but you need to be smart here."

"You don't need to worry. It was just one drink." "Lou, that man has a hold on you," she said sternly.

I couldn't help but be irritated by her reaction. I knew she meant well. She'd had to pick up the pieces last time I'd seen Zack. But I was a different person now. She should have more faith in me. "I can look after myself," I snapped.

"I'm sorry." She reached over and grabbed my leg. "I just care about you. I know you're a strong woman."

I squeezed her hand. "No, I'm sorry. I know you're just looking out for me. This week has just been *a lot."*

She looked over at me sympathetically. "So, are you seeing him again?"

"On Thursday," I mumbled.

I led back against the sofa, staring at the ceiling, replaying Kayleigh's words over and over in my head. She was right, but I didn't want her to be.

Zack did have a hold on me. He always had. Everything stopped when we were together, regardless of who might be in the firing line.

The rest of the week went slow, I had so much anticipation over mine and Zack's next meeting, and I had little to distract myself from it. I had no work to do to keep my mind occupied, so was filling the days absentmindedly watching The Real Housewives, allowing the drama and luxury of their lives to send me into a perfect world of escapism.

Eventually, Thursday came around, and there were only a few hours standing between him and me. I decided to have a bath to both pass the time and calm myself down.

My hair had been scraped up into a bun on the top of my head for days to hide the grease that was mounting, and I also needed to shave my legs as I was beginning to resemble a Wookie.

I turned on the tap and put my hand under it until the water became almost too hot; and poured the remains of a citrus bubble bath into the steaming water.

My dressing gown slipped off my shoulders and dipped my toe into the water, retracting when the heat contacted my skin. I got into the bath, laying my head against the ceramic, my feet hanging over the edge of the bath.

The water and bubbles wrapped around me like a safe, warm cocoon that I never wanted to leave. I stared at the sunflower tattoo on my wrist, letting my mind run away from me, and the memories consume me, reminiscing on all the times I had shared with Zack, good and bad—when Maeve, Alex, Zack and I were in our little bubble, carefree and happy before life had dealt us all such a bad hand.

It was still the happiest time of my life, but remembering it was so painful for so many reasons. I wished we could all go back in time more than anything.

If I was going to keep seeing Zack, to let him back in, it was time to face up to all the pain that had occurred over the last few years. I had tried so hard to move on and be happy again, and for the most part, I was, but there was always a lingering dull ache in my soul that I couldn't shake. I knew I couldn't harbour these negative feelings towards Zack any longer if I was to ever fully heal. I had to forgive him, maybe we could be friends, or maybe we would never see each other again, but at least I would have closure.

I had to say my piece.

Louise 2012

It had been a few weeks since our night at crazy golf. Maeve, Alex, Zack and I had been virtually inseparable since. We'd been enjoying the warm summer evenings after work, going for drinks, watching films together with a takeaway and going for picnics on the top of the hill at the park.

At first, I was worried our conversation in the car had freaked him out, and he thought I was too damaged, but the bond we had formed over the last few weeks proved that theory wrong.

I was nervous the next time I saw him at Maeve's a few days after. We had been watching a film together. My body was unsure where to put my hand and how to sit with him sitting next to me, nervous I would breathe too loud or have a double chin.

When he put his arm around me pulling me close, I could hear his heart beating and feel his hand on my skin. The next few weeks were spent texting all day, staying up until the early hours of the morning on the phone and late-night drives. We had spoken about everything; from whether we believed in aliens to our hopes for the future.

The cuddling continued during our group movie nights, kisses on the forehead, play fighting, any excuse we could to touch each other… but nothing more.

I had zero experience with the opposite sex, so I wasn't sure what the signals were for if someone liked you. My head was confused, unsure if he just saw me as a best friend or if there was more to it, but I knew that being confused and having him in my life was better than him not being in my life at all.

It was a Saturday afternoon, and I was packing my bag to head to Maeve's house. Her Mum and Dad were away, so we were going to watch some films and stay the night. My mind was racing over the possibilities of where we would sleep and the potential the night had.

When I arrived, the others were debating over what food to order, a series of menus spread across the large
kitchen island for guidance.

Maeve's house was in the best part of town, a grand detached house where everything inside was high tech and sparkly. I'd always preferred hanging out at Maeve's than my own.

"Let's ask Lou. She can be the decider," Alex chimed as I took a seat on one of the bar chairs. "Pizza or Chinese?"

"Whatever everyone else fancies." I shrugged.

My eating had got better. I made myself sick less and less

over the past few weeks. Maybe because became more and more enamoured with Zack, I'm not sure. But regardless, I still didn't care much for eating greasy food, especially in front of other people.

"Lou, you have to decide," Alex groaned.

I could see Zack's face in my peripheral vision, his face twisted, watching me intently.

"Chinese then," I said firmly.

"Chinese it is." Alex smiled, grateful that debate was over.

"Alex and I will go collect it. You two pick a film," Maeve smiled.

Ugh, she'd been trying everything she could to get Zack and me alone together.

Grabbing her purse and keys, she followed Alex out of the room. "See you in a bit," she called before the sound of the front door slammed behind them.

I turned around to see Zack staring at me. His eyes twinkled, a slight smile on his face.

"Shall, uh, shall we go pick a film then?" I stuttered.

He nodded, following me through to the lounge, the smile still on his face. I sat on the large L-shaped grey sofa right in the corner, my favourite spot.

Zack sat next to me, leaving no room between us. He kept his eyes focused on me as I tried to ignore it, beginning to scroll through the movie channels.

"Zack, what are you looking at?" I snapped after several

minutes of him staring.

He let out a loud laugh at my irritation. "Sorry." He kept laughing. "You're really cute when you're flustered,"

"Well, I wouldn't be flustered if you didn't keep staring at me," I continued.

He waved his hand over his face, gaining back his composure. "I was looking at you because you're really pretty."

"Oh, shut up," I could feel my chest and cheeks burning with embarrassment. I was in a hoodie and leggings. This is probably the worst he had seen me look, having bolted here straight from work, I was a sweaty, makeup less troll. I put my hood up in an attempt to hide my face.

He pulled my hood back down, gently it away from my face. "Don't." I felt his fingers brush my hand as he went to hold it whilst his other hand grazed my cheek. He tilted his head, moving his lips closer to mine. He paused, seeking silent permission with his eyes.

My stomach was doing somersaults. I had been waiting for this moment since the night we met. I nodded slowly, unable to get a word out. Zack's hand moved down to my chin, he pulled me closer as he leaned into me.

I closed my eyes, feeling his lips graze mine. My heart stopped, time stopped, and suddenly I was whole. I felt his tongue softly enter my mouth, slowly moving against mine. My hand moved into his hair, pulling him into me. Inexperience overruled by instinct, my body somehow knew exactly what to do.

I felt Zack pull away, and I lingered where his lips had been, not wanting the moment to end. I opened my eyes slowly and looked up at him.

"I've waited a long time to kiss you," he said softly. He leaned in again, kissing me gently before pulling further away, leaning back against the couch. The smile on his face was too much to bare.

He grabbed the remote from my hand. "How about a horror?" He began surfing through the channels as if the kiss had never happened.

"Sure." I coughed, looking at the TV.

Alex and Maeve arrived back not long after with two large bags of food, spreading them out on the lounge floor. We ate the Chinese whilst watching Wrong Turn, neither me nor Zack saying another word about what had happened.

"I'm ready for bed," Maeve announced at around midnight. We'd watched almost three films by then, and we were all fighting to stay awake. "You can both go in the spare room, or there is the sofa bed if you don't want to share," she continued, waiting for Alex to pull her up off the sofa.

I didn't look at Zack. I quickly made my way up the stairs bolting for the door of the spare room without so much as a night to Maeve and Alex.

I could hear his footsteps following me as I entered the room, I walked next to the bed unsure what to say in order to hide the face I was freaking out inside.

Zack walked in and closed the door gently behind him.

"Is this okay? I don't mind sleeping on the floor?" he asked.

"No, it's fine. We can share," I gulped, trying not to show how nervous I was.

"You'll regret that once you realise how badly I snore," he smirked. I appreciated his attempt to lighten the mood but remained quiet, unable to muster a sentence together.

"I'm sorry I kissed you earlier, I don't want you to think I'm assuming anything is going to happen here. I respect you more than that Lou."

"I wanted you to kiss me," I whispered. "Do you regret it?" Mortified at the idea, he'd put his lips against mine.

Zack stepped towards me pulling my head into his chest, "Of course, I don't regret it you dick head, I told you I had wanted to do it for ages and I'd kiss you a million more times if I could,"

"Really?" I sounded pathetic but my mind was now mush.

He placed his thumb and forefinger on my chin and pulled it up so that my eyes met his as our breathing began to synchronise. He leant down and kissed me softly.

My desire for him outweighed any nervousness I had. I wrapped my arms around his neck, kissing him back with full force.

He reached for the bottom of my hoodie and began lifting it from my body. I raised my arms, letting him pull it over my head. His eyes were locked on mine, almost silently checking if I was okay with every move he made. I reached over to him, tracing my fingers up his chest and pulling his t-shirt from his body, to reassure him this was exactly what I wanted. He took over, removing it with one arm.

I pulled off my leggings, trying not to trip over as they came off my ankles. I stood in front of him, barer and more vulnerable than I had ever been with anyone before. I put my hands over my body, suddenly feeling so exposed.

"Louise, we can stop whatever this is now if you're not comfortable, it's okay?"

"No, I want to". If I didn't do this now I never would, and I had never even wanted to have sex with anyone and now I had the opportunity to do it with Zack.

Zack continued, taking off his jeans, watching me the whole time. His body was perfect, muscles perfectly defined, but not too big.

He grabbed my arms pulling them away from my body. I felt his eyes looking over me and smiled sweetly. "You are perfect, Louise." His lips kissed my collarbone, and up my neck. Then he picked me up with ease and placed me on top of the bed. "We can stop at any time Lou, okay? Just say if you change your mind". He waited till I nodded in conformation.

"Have you had sex before?" His voice was firm and confident.

"No." I shook my head, too intoxicated in him to be

embarrassed.

"If it hurts at any point, you need to tell me." He remained serious.

I nodded in response, bracing myself. I felt his fingers slip into my underwear, and I gasped at his touch.

"Does that feel good?" he murmured in my ear. I nodded again, letting out a moan I had no control over as his fingers moved inside me. He moved down my body, pulling my legs further apart, his eyes on me as my body reacted to his touch. My head lent back and my back

arched at the euphoria I was experiencing as his fingers moved against my body. I moaned his name as his fingers circled my clitoris, sending me dizzy. He removed his fingers to my annoyance, I felt empty without his fingers inside me, I looked up at him pouting.

"That was just the start, Lou." He smouldered as he reached into his jean pocket to pull out a condom from his wallet. I rejoiced at the thought. He edged himself inside me slowly, and he looked at me the whole time, checking I was okay.

I gasped as my body felt a twinge of pain, feeling the difference of his girth from his fingers. I grabbed his arm for support.

"Shall I stop?" his face was full of concern.

"No, keep going."

Our bodies moved in time as the pain lessened and the feeling of pleasure took over."

"Louise, you are so beautiful," Zack whispered in my ear as I bit his shoulder, trying to stifle my moans. I felt Zack's body stiffen as his pleasure mounted, and he let out a moan as he released himself into me.

I stared up at the ceiling as Zack moved his body off mine, lost in a state of ecstasy.

"Are you okay?" Zack turned towards me, kissing me softly on the shoulder.

"Yes," I smiled at him before moving into his embrace. "It was perfect,"

"You deserve only the best Miss Moore, I'm just happy I could be a part of it."

Louise Present Day

I arrived at the restaurant and walked inside, hearing the loud hum of the other customers filling the small, overcrowded room. It was a family-run Italian restaurant in the area. I had been here a few times and the red and white patch tablecloths and heavily accented waiters always drew me back.

I spotted the back of Zack's head across the room, and gestured to the server where I was headed before walking over to the dimly lit corner. I slid into the seat opposite him before he could get up to greet me.

"Well, hi there," he said. "You look…. Wow." He gulped as he eyed me up and down.

I was glad he had noticed. I couldn't pretend I hadn't tried to make an effort. He could only see the top half of me over the table, but it was enough. My black corseted dress clung perfectly over what little breasts I had. I'd managed to smooth my hair into a fifties style Hollywood curl, tucking one side behind my ear, exposing my collar bones. I may have come here with honourable intentions, but I couldn't deny it was satisfying to know he was undressing me with his eyes.

"Hey." I smirked at him as I clocked him looking at my cleavage. He looked back up to my face and flushed red. "How are you?" His voice was deep and serious.

"I'm good. How are you?"

"Good, thanks," he gulped, "I'm glad you wanted to see me again."

"I had a nice time the other night." The atmosphere was different tonight, heavy and full of tension.

"I've ordered a bottle for us." He smiled.

"Perfect."

The waiter brought over a bottle of wine in an ice bucket and began filling the glasses. Zack and I didn't break eye contact the whole time.

"Thank you," he said to the waiter, still looking at me. "Do you know what's changed the most about you?" he began.

"No, what?" I suddenly became very self-conscious, trying to think about what had drastically changed about me since we'd last seen each other.

"You seem so much more… I don't know, confident?" He took a sip out of his glass. "It looks good on you."

I smiled awkwardly and brushed my hair back behind my ears.

He was right. He had only ever known me as a broken, shy girl. And, sure, part of her was still there, but everything that had happened over the last few years had helped me accept myself for who I really was.

"Thank you."

"Are you, erm, still… Are you better?" He trailed off. "I'm fine… I don't... anymore," I said, trying not to say the words. "It's been a long time since I've felt like I needed to do that."

It was half true, I hadn't done it in a long time, but the urge hadn't gone, especially of late.

He looked relieved with my answer, and the tension in his face disappeared.

We ordered a pizza to share as we caught each other up on the years missed, laughing and hanging on to each other's every word. Sharing old stories about our summer with Maeve and Alex, it felt just how it had then, easy.

As the drinks flowed and my inhibitions lowered, the wholesome stories drifted back into the past as I was brought back to the present as my insurmountable lust for him crept through my body.

I knew I should put the food down and leave, this was a dangerous place to be, drunk and lusting after a man I had loved for so long. But I didn't. My head was no match for my heart. I stayed, watching his eyes explore my body, neither of us was listening to the other. I wanted to be alone with him, but I knew I had to be sensible.

"You need to eat more," Zack said when he saw me playing with my second piece of pizza.

"I'm full," I replied.

"Well, Louise, we are not leaving until you eat at least one more slice." He raised his eyebrows, challenging me.

"Who made you the boss?" I couldn't pretend I didn't like it.

"I'm just looking after you, that's all." His face turned serious before he put another slice of pizza on my plate and looked at me expectantly.

I finished my pizza obediently, feeling his gaze on me the whole time. I washed it down with the rest of my wine. When I had finished my third slice, I looked up at him, searching for approval.

"Okay. Now we can go." He smirked. "Shall we go back to mine? I've got another bottle at home?" Zack looked at me hungrily, and it sounded more like an instruction than a question.

"Sure."

I was reminded of Kayleigh's warning, but I shook it off as I stood up and followed him out of the restaurant, my curiosity taking over. We walked side by side back to his place, a sense of danger and desire lingering in the pit of my stomach.

The tension between us built as we went up the stairs of his building towards his front door.

I entered his flat, curious to see what his world looked like.

The walls were exposed brick. Large house plants were placed in jewel-tone pots at every corner and a large L shaped leather sofa dominated the room.

It was exactly how you would imagine a city bachelor pad— but with hints of Zack's personality dotted around; large pieces of art, stacks of games and photos of him and his family.

He motioned for me to take a seat on the sofa as he went to get the bottle of wine from his kitchen counter.

We both knew that our inhibitions were now low enough to finally address all the things we'd been ignoring, and we needed to keep the alcohol coming if we were to talk about our past. If we didn't do it now, the occasion might never arise again.

I had come here tonight to find a way to forgive him, and now was the time, I couldn't stay hating him for another 10 years, my soul needed to heal.

He took a seat next to me, handing me the glass before locking eyes with me. "I think it's time we just lay all our cards on the table." He looked at me as if he knew what I had been thinking.

I took a sip of wine out of my glass for courage. "Well…" I gulped. "You broke my heart, you know. More than once." I could feel the decade of unsaid words boiling inside me.

"I know." He sighed. "I never wanted to. I just tried to do what was best for everyone. Please don't think that I didn't care about you. I have never stopped."

I broke our eye contact. I didn't want him to see the pain in my eyes.

"That night, when you left, I was ready to give it all up for you. Just things got in the way."

"What things?" I demanded.

"Things that don't matter anymore. I'm sorry, I know I've put you through so much. I wanted to contact you, but you told me to never speak to you again.

"I wasn't sure how you would react if I had reached out. I was a coward." He looked at me, searching my face for answers I didn't have.

Part of me wished he'd tried to win me back, but the other part of me knew that I was in such a dark place at the time. I probably wouldn't have reacted well.

"What happened with you and Chris?" he eventually said.

"You happened." I looked down at the wine in my glass. "He couldn't forgive me, and I can't blame him. He deserved a lot better than me." My stomach ached with the guilt I felt every time I was reminded of him.

"That's not true, Lou. You deserve the world.
It's me who messed it up for you."

"No. I'm the one who betrayed him." I Paused. "What between you and Grace?"

"We stayed together for a few months." He winced. "We'd been in a bad place anyway. Some other things happened, and eventually, it all just came crashing down. It was only a matter of time before we ended."

I felt relieved, knowing she was no longer someone I needed to worry about. It was just him and me after all this time.

"How have you been since…"

I cut him off, "Let's not talk about her. Please." I wasn't ready for that conversation.

"Sorry" he paused. "Well, what about now? Is there anyone else?"

"No. You?"

"No."

I took another sip of wine. "Okay, cards on the table." I gulped, knowing what I was about to say was a loaded question. "Did you ever really love me?"

"Yes, more than you could ever know." His eyes were genuine, and I wanted to believe him. "I regret everyday how I treated you. You didn't deserve that, and I will always wonder what if?" He paused, "Do you…ever wonder?"

"Yes." I whispered.

He stared at me. He didn't look scared or phased by my reply. Instead, an animalistic look came over him. I had seen that look once before, and I knew exactly what it meant.

His hand reached out and took my glass from my grasp, placing it on the table in front of us. He turned back towards me, moving his body closer, pushing me back onto the sofa. I could feel his weight on top of me as he made his way to my head.

Our eyes met, he stayed still, staring into my soul. "Cards on the table?" he whispered. I nodded breathlessly. "I've thought about you, kissing you, touching you, and loving you every day for the last two years." His eyes scanned my lips. I could smell the alcohol on his breath. He moved his mouth onto mine and kissed me deeply.

I kissed him back. Hard. His kiss instantly deepened, his tongue moved against mine, and we were both hooked. His fingers made their way up my body and into my hair, his other hand ran along my thigh up inside my dress. Our bodies touched each other effortlessly, remembering each other's rhythm.

His tongue found its way to the top of my breasts as he pulled down the straps of my dress, exploring his way down to my nipples.

I pushed against his body, driving his back against the sofa as I moved on top of him. I could feel how much he wanted me through his jeans. Any reservations I had disappeared, and I wanted him more than anything. I unbuckled his belt and undid his jeans, pulling him inside me, desperate to feel his touch again. He groaned as I moved against his body, clinging onto me to pull me in closer. His head was buried in my hair, and my fingers were digging in his back as we found our rhythm.

"I need you, Lou", he whispered in my ear as we moaned, finishing in unison. Neither of us moved. We laid there breathlessly.

Drunk on each other.

Louise 2012

I was over at Maeve's helping her pack. She was moving in two weeks. I sat on her bed, and she threw a pile of dresses at me to fold as she continued to decide what to take.

"So, yeah, I think me and Alex will be fine," she concluded. She'd been talking for the last hour about how she and Alex wouldn't succumb to the uni relationship curse, and that they'd be fine with a little distance.

I wasn't sure if she was trying to convince herself or me, but I nodded, amused by her fretting. I knew they'd be okay. They were head over heels for each other.

"What about you and Zack, anyway?" She whipped her head around, looking at me, stifling a laugh.

"What about Zack and me?"

"Well, has he said anything about what happened? Are you together now?"

I smiled. "We haven't discussed it," but we'd been in each

other's pockets since. "We are just friends." I laughed.

"Friends, my arse," she snuffed. She continued sorting through her wardrobe, tossing clothes around the room. "So, have you thought any more about London?"

"Yeah, I had a chat with Dad about it," I said. A week or so after that night in the car with Zack, I had spoken to Dad about uni. It went a lot better than I ever could have imagined, Dad practically dialled the phone himself for me to work something out with the university. Thankfully, because I had only just got my results, they were happy for me to start on the next cohort.

"And?" she pressed.

"They're letting me start in January," I continued.

Maeve grinned back at me and jumped onto me, cuddling me. "Your Mum would be so proud of you, Lou." She held me tight and kissed my forehead.

"We laid there looking up at the ceiling, enjoying each other's company, knowing we wouldn't be able to do this again for a while. "Have you told Zack?"

"Not yet, but he's always said I should go to London, so I'm sure he'll be happy for me." Truthfully, I hadn't thought about how it might affect him and me. "I know it means me moving, but it's only a train away. We can do what you and Alex are doing, right?"

"Exactly, and until you go, you can all just come and visit me in Leeds." She beamed.

"And interrupt your and Alex's sex fest?"

She kicked me, and we erupted into laughter. "Right, come on, dick head, we need to get ready to meet the boys."

Maeve got up and headed for the shower just as my phone buzzed. I picked it up. It was Zack.

I've got you a present.

I beamed.

What is it?!

He replied instantly.

You'll have to wait and see.

It had been a perfect summer day, with a light breeze and a soft cloud over the sky. We'd decided to all go up the hill at the back of the town park, have some drinks, and enjoy the mid-afternoon sun.

Alex had brought a football and was playfully teaching Maeve to dribble the ball. Zack and I lay on the grass, watching the clouds pass by.

He turned to look at me. "You look nice in a dress." "I think you'd look nice in a dress too," I teased.

He laughed, throwing a handful of grass at me. "So, my new boss rang. I start next Monday," he said.

"That's amazing! Are you excited?"

“Yeah, I feel like my life is about to start,” He sat up and reached for his bag. “Do you want your present?”

“Hell yeah.” I twisted around, so I was laying on my stomach to face him. He pulled an A4 envelope out of his bag and handed it to me. “What is it?” I asked curiously.

“Open it and you’ll see.”

I opened the envelope's flap and slid out a piece of card from inside. I flipped over the paper and gasped, putting a hand over my mouth.

It was me.

He had drawn me, except he had drawn me in a way I had never seen myself before; I looked beautiful. My hair was tucked behind my ears, and I was smiling, a glisten in my eye. He’d drawn me holding a book with the title of my novel. He’d surrounded me in sunflowers, my favourite.

A tear fell and dropped down my cheek as he reached over and wiped it away. “Do you like it?” he asked.

“Zack—,” I was speechless. “I love it. I look so…”

“You look like you, Lou. You just don’t see yourself the way everyone else does.”

“Thank you. This is honestly the nicest thing anyone has ever done for me.”

“It’s okay. You deserve to see yourself this way.” He smiled. “I even drew your tattoo.” He pointed to the picture of a tiny sunflower on the inside of my wrist. I got it last week. Zack had taken me to the city to see his new tattoo place. He’d introduced me to his boss, Ollie—a mid-30s, tall, slim man who was covered head to toe in tattoos.

"It's company policy that the apprentice has to get a tattoo," Ollie challenged.

"Only if Lou gets one too." Zack looked at me, waiting for me to dismiss his dare.

"Fine," I said boldly, his eyes widening in surprise. "But I get to pick yours, and you can pick mine."

"Deal."

I chose a crescent moon for him, as every time the moon was out, he would tell me all about the meaning of the moon phase.

He chose a sunflower for me. "You love sunflowers, and you remind me of one..." He placed a firm kiss on my head.

"Have you met me? I'm dark and moody," I joked.

"Nah, I see the real you. The dark and moody is all an act."

I stuck my middle finger at him. I loved the tattoo, though, and every time I looked at it, it reminded me to be the me that Zack saw.

"Oi, you two, what you talking about?" Alex shouted as they made their way up the hill. I put the picture in my bag, not wanting to share it with anyone else.

"Hey guys, did you see my mad football skills?" Maeve re-enacted her dribble for us.

"Bambi on the ice more like." Alex grabbed her as she playfully pulled him to the ground.

"So, has Lou told you her big news?" Maeve asked once she caught her breath.

I glared at her. I had meant to tell Zack, but I wanted to do it when it was just us two.

"No?" Zack turned towards me, a crinkly between his brows.

"Yeah, so… I've been meaning to tell you. I am going to London for uni in January." I saw Zack's eyes change, his face dropped.

"That's amazing, Lou!" Alex exclaimed, he hadn't clocked Zack's reaction, but I could see Maeve's eyes darting between the two of us.

Zack flinched, and his face changed to a smile as he pulled me in for a hug. "Well done, Lou. I'm happy for you."

I was relieved. For a second, I thought he was mad at me.

We stayed in the park as the sun set, feeling the buzz from the vodka clouding my brain. Zack hadn't said anything more about me going to London and was acting completely normal with me. We spent the night laughing harder than we had all summer. I think we all knew it was probably the last time we'd all be together like this.

The sky was almost pitch black by the time we decided to head home. Maeve and Alex strolled off in the opposite direction holding hands, savouring every last moment together.

"Come on, let's go," Zack said abruptly, already walking away. I jogged to catch up with him, making me realise how tipsy I was. I linked my arm through his to use him as a support.

"Why didn't you tell me, Lou? About London."

"Oh, well, I was going to, but Maeve beat me to it." He didn't say anything. "I'm sorry."

He shook his head as if shaking off whatever thoughts were running through his head. "No, don't be silly. I'm so happy for you and proud of you for taking the leap." He slipped his arm out of mine and put it around my shoulders instead, pulling me in and kissing me on the head. "I'm just going to miss you."

"You'll see me all the time, I can come to visit on weekends, and you can visit me when you aren't working. Anyway, I'm not leaving for a few more months." I was rambling. I knew I was just speaking my thoughts out loud as I, too, was trying to work out how we could make this work.

"Yeah, sure we can," he replied unconvincingly.

We continued walking towards mine. The air was heavy with tension. We approached my house, and I lingered, knowing something was changing between us. He lingered, too.

He pulled me close to him and buried his face in my hair, mine in his chest. I could smell the alcohol on both of us and the warmth it was giving us.

"Lou." He pulled his head away, still holding me.

I didn't want to look at him. I wanted to stay buried in his chest forever. I was safe here. He put his hands around my face and moved my head to face him. His eyes looked full of sadness, but they were looking right through me.

He leaned in, and I closed my eyes as I felt his lips graze mine cautiously.

I grabbed his jacket and pulled him in, kissing him with no hesitation, my lips firm on his as I pushed my tongue into his mouth. I could feelhis whole body relax at my kiss. He put his hand round the back of my neck, pulling me in as close as he could.

We couldn't put our feelings into words, but we could show it to each other.

"Lou," he breathed heavily between kisses. I moved my hands up his body and placed them on either side of his face, immersing myself in him. He jolted, going limp. He grabbed my hands and kissed them before pulling them anyway. "I'm sorry. I can't do this." He leaned in and kissed me on the forehead, holding his lips there a second too long. "I'm sorry. Night, Lou."

He turned away and walked down the street. I stood there watching him walk away as tears fell down my face, unsure of what just happened.

All I knew was, something had changed.

I just hoped it wasn't forever.

Louise Present Day

My eyes opened to the orange hue of the sunrise filling the bedroom. The air was fresh, the open white curtains gently moved in the morning breeze, making its way through the ajar window.

The room smelt like sex and wine. I stretched my limbs and rolled onto my side, facing the window, my back turned to Zack. I looked out the window, a mother magpie bringing food back to her babies in the nest buried in the corner of the building. I embraced what I saw, knowing I was experiencing the calm before the storm.

My stomach felt tight, my body was going into fight-or-flight mode. Knowing what history had taught me, my heart was about to get broken, and I needed to prepare for the impact. I let myself drift back to sleep,
allowing my body to sink into the bed. It was safer there than reality.

"Lou?" A hand traced over my waist, up to my arm and

then to my neck, pulling my hair behind my back.

I felt a soft kiss on my shoulder.

I opened my eyes. My body clenched in autopilot, fearful of the next few moments when I realised he wasn't running; he was kissing my shoulder and running his hand up and down my arm.

I turned over to face him. He looked puffy and swollen from being freshly woken, innocent, his curls framing his face. He looked down and smiled at me as my eyes met his.

"Morning," my voice was croaky, and my mouth was dry from the wine. I was not a morning person, and no amount of gorgeous man lying next to me was going to change that. "What time is it?" I groaned.

"Half nine. I have to go to work at one, so I have time to make us some breakfast if you want to stay?" He seemed nervous, as if he was worried I might be the one doing the running this time.

"Yeah, that sounds nice. But let's just lie here for a while."

He put his arms around me and pulled me in, resting his chin on my head. He kissed me on the head and pulled me in closer, tracing shapes onto my thigh with his finger. I closed my eyes again, hoping this moment would last forever.

Eventually, reality resumed, and a loud buzz came from the bedside table. He let go of me and turned over.

I immediately felt exposed and vulnerable as his touch left my body. He read the message. I wondered who it was, realising I knew little about his life now; who were his friends, who did he date, was the text from his mum?

"Sorry, just needed to check it wasn't work." His mouth twitched as if there was something else he wanted to say. He went to get out of bed. "How about that breakfast?"

"Sure." I watched as he stood up and stretched. The muscles in his back were perfectly defined. It was one of the only parts that weren't covered in tattoos.

He pulled on his boxers and made his way out of the bedroom. I rolled onto my back, reeling over the events of the night before.

I wasn't sure what I had learned, he had loved me? He wasn't freaking out about us? I was more confused than ever before.

I turned over and grabbed my phone, and saw a message from Kayleigh flash on the screen.

How was last night?? Spill the tea!!

I'll reply later, I thought. I didn't need an interrogation this early in the morning.

I moved to the edge of the bed, looking around the room for my underwear, which I saw hanging from a chair in the corner of the room. I stood up, retrieving my pants before pulling them on and one of Zack's t-shirts off the top of a pile of fresh washing, and made my way back to the kitchen.

The hallway filled with the sound of Paulo Nutini playing

in the background. Zack was singing along in the kitchen, slicing up some avocado on a wooden chopping board. He looked so free and happy. I hadn't seen him like this for a long time.

I walked over to the breakfast bar and took a seat on the stool, watching him, amused. He looked up and smiled at me, and started dancing towards me.

"What are you doing?" I laughed. "You dance like my Dad!" I laughed loudly as he continued towards me, moving his arms and clicking along to the beat of the song.

"Dance with me, Mademoiselle."

I cackled at him. He looked ridiculous.

He reached his hands out, and I reluctantly went along with it. He spun me around the kitchen, dipping me to the floor and kissing me in between laughs.

The music changed to a slow song, and he pulled me close to him, slowly swaying me. The laughs stopped, and I gave into him, burying my head in his chest.

"You know what, I think it's finally our time," he whispered.

I grabbed him as tight as I could. I had waited almost a decade for this, for the pieces to finally fall into place, for the universe to finally let us be together. We were older, wiser and ready to make this work. It was our time.

*

I arrived back at my flat around noon, as close to the time that Zack needed to go to work as possible. I didn't want to leave. I didn't want to burst our little bubble. My phone buzzed. It was Kayleigh.

Be over in 10. Need to get you to sign some papers.

I laughed internally. I knew she had ulterior motives to come over, and I knew as happy as she'd be I'd finally had sex, she would be less than thrilled about who it was with.

Right on cue, ten minutes later, there was a knock on the door, and Kayleigh let herself in.

"Hey babe, just some quick things to sign." She walked straight into the living area and over to the kitchen table, pulling a manila envelope out of her bag and placing it on the table.

I stood up and went over to the table, signing obediently. I could see her watching me like a hawk, trying to read my face for information.

"So…" she finally began. "How was the big meeting with your lover boy?"

Here we go, I thought. "It was good, thanks."

"Okay, cut the crap. Tell me what happened." She pulled out the chair from under the table and took a seat, waiting for me to divulge.

I sighed. "Okay, we had a great time, had a lovely dinner, got some things off of our chests." I took a deep breath, "and we had sex." I glanced over to gauge her reaction. She remained poised, and said nothing. "I know you think I'm stupid, but it's not like how it used to be. We spoke this morning, and we've both agreed the time is right for us to finally give this a go properly," I continued to ramble.

Her silence made me nervous. I knew I had to convince her that this was a good idea, and honestly, I think I still needed to convince myself, too, because in that moment it felt like a dream that I might wake up from at any moment.

I could tell she was mulling over how to best approach this. She could come across as brash and honest at times, and she knew she needed to be careful with what she said.

"Okay." She paused, recollecting her thoughts. "Do you think he's changed?"

"Yes, I really do. This morning just felt different." "Okay, and is Grace still in the picture at all?"

"No. He said it ended after what happened," I looked at her hopefully. I needed her to be on my side here.

"Okay." She paused. "Well, Lou, if you're happy, that's all that matters." She leaned over and hugged me.

I knew this was her way of showing her concern, and telling me she was there for me when it went wrong. But it wasn't going to go wrong this time. I was sure of it.

"So, how was the sex?" She nudged me playfully.
"Amazing. It felt right." I could feel my cheeks flushing red. "This morning was better, though. It all just fell into place. There was no

drama, no regret… just perfection."

"Well, I'm glad he's not fucked you over again." She grimaced. "I'm happy for you, I really am," she quickly added.

I smiled and let it go. She wasn't wrong, he had fucked me over multiple times now, and I'm sure she thought I was just blindly believing everything he was telling me, but I knew Zack. He rarely said how he felt, so I knew he meant it when he opened up.

Kayleigh and I spent the afternoon catching up, her telling me about her date and the fact she had also seen the waiter again for a night of passion.

Not long after she left, my phone pinged.

I'll be done with work around 6. Free tonight? I could bring over some dinner. Been thinking about you all day x

I smiled as I read the message on my phone and began replying to Zack.

Sounds good to me. See you later x

I put my phone down and looked around my flat, realising that it was a complete shit hole.

I got to work, stripping the bed and putting on fresh sheets and collecting up the dirty clothes from various rooms and put them in the laundry basket. I cleaned the kitchen, throwing out any spoiled food that I hadn't gotten round to eating, wiping the surfaces and taking out the bin.

I went for a shower and threw on a big green jumper and some grey joggers. One perk of seeing Zack again was that he knew exactly what I looked like, but that didn't mean I wanted to show off my body to him.

I went through the flat, lighting candles and turning down the lights to create ambience. I pulled the arm onto my record player and let the music fill the flat.

The summer had blessed us with a continued spell of warm weather, so I opened the floor to ceiling window at the back of my living area to let the warm air filter in.

I looked around and laughed to myself about how I'd made my flat look like a sex den.

I quickly turned the lights back on.

The buzzer went off, and I made my way over to the intercom to let Zack in.

I opened the door and waited for him to make his way up the stairs. He came round the corner, his face lighting up when he saw me waiting for him in the doorway.

He was carrying two large bags of Chinese in one hand and a crate of beers in the other.

He leant down and kissed me as he approached.

"Satay chicken?" I asked.

"Of course."

I grabbed the bags out of his hands and showed him through to the living area. My mind went back to the last time we had a Chinese together; the night he took my virginity, I got butterflies just thinking about it. I put the food on the coffee table and headed to the kitchen to grab the bottle opener.

"This flat is so you," he said as he was pacing through the room, looking at all my stuff.

"What do you mean?"

"I don't know… it's just your personality. Full of books, weird gothic ornaments, and artwork."

"Is that a good thing?"

"Absolutely, it's unapologetically you. I love it, a lot going on, in the best way." He came towards me and hugged me with one arm, tapping me on the head with his other hand. "Lots of things going on in here too."

"And that's where they will stay," I said, playfully pushing him off me.

I sat on my large velvet sofa and opened the pizza boxes as he sat down next to me, opening two beers.

"How was work?" I asked, reaching over to grab a slice of pizza, being careful to catch the cheese before it dripped anywhere.

"Good, was finishing off a large chest piece. How was your day? What have you been doing?"

I sat on my large velvet sofa and opened the food boxes as he sat down next to me, opening two beers.

"How was work?" I asked, reaching over to grab a fork full of noodles being careful to catch them in my mouth before they dropped anywhere.

"Good, was finishing off a large chest piece. How was your day? What have you been doing?"

"Not much, Kayleigh came over." "Ah, is she still your agent?"

"Agent, best friend."

"Bet she loved this, didn't she?" He gestured between us both, looking concerned.

"She was happy for us, actually," I lied.

His face relaxed. "Good. I wouldn't blame her if she did hate me after the last time though. I wouldn't blame you, either."

"I don't hate you. I never have." I took a swig of beer from the bottle. I never hated him as much as I wanted to. I knew he wasn't a bad person deep down.

"Well, I'm glad you have someone to fill the best friend roll." He smiled a genuine, warm smile that reached his eyes.

Was he alluding to the gap Maeve had left?

"Me too," I murmured.

Zack reached for another slice before continuing. "I'm seeing Alex next weekend, actually." He paused nervously. "Do you want to come?" He seemed unsure.

I continued eating, pondering his question. I had only seen Alex a handful of times over the last few years, and it was always awkward and weird. We occasionally texted, checking in, but the friendship had faded.

"Actually, yeah. I would like to see him." Maybe it would be easier to have Zack there, less pressure on Alex and me to find some common ground.

"Actually, yeah. I would like to see him." Maybe it would be easier to have Zack there, less pressure on Alex and me to find some common ground.

He gleamed. "Great. He'll be so happy to see you. And he will love that we are talking through things. I want us to be together. Properly."

I beamed as he said the words. I was relieved his feelings hadn't changed once he left the bubble this morning. "You do?"

"Yes." He looked sternly at me. "I know it seems fast, Lou, but it's not. I have wanted you to be mine for almost ten years, and now it's all or nothing. We have waited long enough, don't you think?"

I was taken aback by how serious he was. I didn't want to point out that we could have been together a lot sooner if it wasn't for him, but something told me I shouldn't question this. He was being so vulnerable with me, and now was not the time to ruin it.

"I hope I'm worth the wait," I said.

"You are." His face relaxed again, and he pulled me on top of him, kissing me all over. "You are everything I have ever wanted." He kissed me hard, with purpose.

His hand began tickling my spine, tracing under my jumper pulling it up over my head and began kissing my breasts and nipples as I moaned with his touch. He picked me up and carried me to the bedroom, gently placing me on the fresh sheets I'd put on earlier that day.

His eyes gazed down at me on the bed. "You were made for me," he whispered. He removed his top with one hand and took off his jeans, looking at me the whole time. I gasped as he moved inside me.

Our bodies were sweaty from the humidity that filled the room, our skin salty to taste. His fingers locked in my hair as he pulled my head back so he could whisper in my ear as he pushed harder inside me.

We lay side by side, catching our breath, Zack encapsulating me in his arms.

"I can't believe I was ever dumb enough to let you go." He held me tighter. "I'm never letting you go, Louise. I won't lose you ag

Louise 2012

It had been over a week since Zack and I had last spoken. I contemplated calling him a few times, but decided against it after he didn't reach out.

Every fibre of my being was hoping he had just been so busy with his new job that he hadn't had the chance to text or call, but I knew deep down it was more than that.

Something had changed in him that night.

Maeve was as confused as I was, she'd been trying to get information from Alex, but he was clueless as will.

We had all arranged to go to Maeve's tonight for a drink as she was leaving in the morning, but I had no idea if he would still be going. I prayed he was.

If it was just about me moving to London, I knew we

could get past it if we just talked it through.

As I approached Maeve's front door, I felt sick to my stomach, praying he would be there and we would go back to normal. Praying that this was all a bad dream that I was about to wake up from.

"Hey, you," Maeve said as she opened the door. "Don't worry, he's not here yet." I sighed with relief. "Have you heard anything from him yet?" she questioned as we walked through the house to the back garden.

"No, nothing."

"Don't let it get to you, Lou. You haven't done anything wrong," she said.

About an hour later, I heard the handle on the back gate move as it was being opened from the other side. Zack walked through, holding a crate of beers and some flowers. He looked at me, gave a small smile, and then looked away quickly to greet Alex and Maeve.

"Take a seat, man," Alex said, gesturing to the chair next to me. Zack handed Maeve the flowers and sat down, he wiped his hands on his thighs and then folded his arms, clearing his throat.

"Hi, Lou. How are you?" His voice was stiff, unnatural.

"I'm good." *What was wrong with him?*

Maeve turned to me with a furrowed brow and screwed up lips.

"So, what did you do last night mate? Me and boys missed you at football," Alex said.

Zack cleared his throat again, his eyes looked down "Erm, I was with a girl actually,"

Maeve turned towards him abruptly with an accusing look. "What?" Maeve demanded, her voice cold, her eyes burning through Zack's body.

His whole body stiffened next to me, and I felt the sting behind my eyes as the tears began building up. I took a deep breath as I fought them back, turning to him and smiling briefly so that he couldn't see my heart breaking right in front of him.

"Oh," Alex said in a high-pitched tone, "how was that?" He asked awkwardly, his eyes widely looking at Maeve for help.

"Yeah, good, thanks mate, she was nice," Zack almost whispered. "How was work?" he added, trying to change the conversation.

He looked at me, there was so much he was trying to say with his eyes, but I looked away before I could get lost in all the things, he was too weak to say to my face.

Alex took the bait and started conversing about his work.

"Excuse me." I stood up and walked away, back into the house.

The pain was too much, and I could feel it working its way through my veins.

I came through the back door into the kitchen and grabbed the family size bag of crisps off of the table and darted to the bathroom before anyone could stop me. I sat on the toilet, shovelling the crips into my mouth, handfuls at a time, the sharp edges cutting my throat from the speed I was eating them.

Once most of the bag had been demolished, I pulled my head back and caught my breath before hunching over the toilet, pushing my fingers into the back of my throat until I felt the sickness coming up through my body.

I leant back and sat on the floor, tears streaming down my eyes.

What the fuck is going on?

Had I imagined this whole thing? Had I just convinced myself that he liked me, when, really,
it was all in my head? Had he just pity kissed me? More importantly—who is this girl he's going on dates with?

I looked down at my wrist, at the yellow sunflower, and stroked it with my finger. It couldn't have all been a lie, could it?

I was pulled out of my trance by the sound of voices. It was Maeve and Alex; I pressed my ear to the door to listen.

"What the fuck is going on? I thought he liked Lou."

"So did I! He's a secretive guy but I never expected him to do this. I'm going to go talk to him, you go see Lou."

"He's such a dick. He's completely led her on. They had sex, for god's sake!" She was spitting her words. "She'll be so upset, and I'm fucking leaving and won't be here to pick up the pieces."

I knew she meant well, but her words stung. Was this how everyone saw me? Just a weak, fragile girl who fell for a guy just because he had been nice to her? A girl who made herself sick and was too scared to leave her Dad?

He didn't want me. He didn't like me. He just felt sorry for me. I turned towards the mirror, wiping the mascara from under my eyes, and faked a smile before walking back out.

Maeve was waiting for me in the hall. "Lou. I'm so sorry. We didn't know."

"It's fine. I'm okay." I tried to speak convincingly, but it didn't work. My voice broke, but she spared me the embarrassment.

"I've just gone absolutely ape-shit at him so you know, Alex is furious too. Her name is Grace. She works at the tattoo shop apparently and she asked him for a drink, he was being VERY defensive." she said, rolling her eyes.

"Makes sense," I said with a sigh. I pictured some leggy brunette with tattoos and piercings, who was equally as intimidating as she was beautiful. Just his type, I was sure.

"I can stay another night if you need me?" Maeve asked, grabbing my hand.

"Don't be silly, I'm fine. I just read too much into it." I squeezed her hand. "You need to go. It's your time to shine." I nudged her with a forced smile.

She glanced at me sadly, trying to force her own smile.

I sat back down next to Zack, he looked at me with regret, but I ignored him. I was in a trance, the next
hour was a blur. My brain was unable to formulate any words., I could feel my body working overtime to go into survival mode.

When the pain got unbearable, I got up to leave. I said goodbye to Maeve, hugging her as tight as possible whilst we both cried in each other's arms.

I knew it would hurt but I hadn't realised just how much until that moment.

I hugged Alex "Please look after her," I whispered in his ear, "make sure she's really okay before you leave,"

As I pulled away from Alex, Maeve made up some excuse for them both to go inside. I turned towards Zack, took a deep breath, and hugged him quickly.

It was an awkward hug, like two strangers who were being forced to interact, avoiding meeting each other's gaze.

He looked surprised as I pulled away. I think maybe he was expecting me to shout at him or something, rather than hug him.

"Lou, I—I don't know what to say," he muttered, looking at his feet.

"Goodbye, Zack," I said firmly.

I left before he could say anymore.

Nothing he could have said would have numbed the pain I was feeling. I knew that was more than just a goodbye.

It was the end.

September

October

November

December

Louise Present Day

I was lovesick. It was official. As soon as a doubt entered my mind, Zack was right there, proving me wrong. He never went longer than a few hours checking in with me, and we never went a day or two without seeing each other.

He was proving my head wrong every step of the way, and in turn, I remembered why he had consumed my heart for all this time.

I felt stupid and childish that it had only been two weeks, and I had let my life fully revolve around him already. I thought as people got older, they were supposed to get smarter. But no, I was here being just as naive as I had been at eighteen—except now I was twenty-seven—and I knew that if I got hurt this time, there was a good chance I would never fully recover.

I grabbed my large purple overnight bag and purse off the

floor, heading out of my flat.

The sun was bright, I took my sunglasses from the top of my head and put them on before heading out the door.

My heart melted as I saw Zack leaning against the car door, sunglasses fading into his chocolate brown hair, a slight shine on his skin. I skipped down the stairs, throwing my bag on the floor as I swung my arms around his neck to greet him.

"I wish everyone was this happy to see me," he said as he wrapped his arms around my back, pulling me up onto my tiptoes.

"I think we would have a serious problem if everyone was this happy to see you," I toyed, pulling myself away and back onto my heels.

"Let me rephrase that. I hope you are always this happy to see me."

I smiled, scrunching my nose at him.

Zack reached down and grabbed my bag, loading it into the boot as I made my way around the car to the passenger's seat. Zack got in, turned on the ignition and put the car into gear, driving down the quiet residential street.

"Are you going to tell me where we are going yet?" I questioned. Zack had told me two days ago that he was taking us on a weekend away, and despite my persistence, he wouldn't tell me where.

"Nope." He turned to me, smiling smugly. *Typical.*

"This is like an episode of Crimewatch. A twenty-seven year old female goes missing after a romantic trip with an ex-lover," I recited, impersonating the voice of a newsreader.

Zack laughed loudly, "It is pretty dumb of you to come with me so blindly now that you mention it." He reached over for my hand and pulled it up to his mouth, kissing it softly. "I'll get rid of the knife at the service station if you're lucky."

"A *knife*!" I mock-gasped. "You couldn't think of a nicer way to murder me? Something less painful, like drugging me or drowning me?"

"Why on earth would you want to drown over being stabbed?" Zack replied, his eyes looked at me wide.

"They say it's like the most painless way to die."

"Yeah, but you would be aware it was
happening. That's awful! At least with a knife, I could make it quick and come from behind so you didn't have to know it was me doing it."

"I want to know you're murdering me… so I can haunt
you.

That way, you'd have to remember the light fading from my eyes for the rest of your life,"

"You're sick." He smirked. "Anyway, you're about to be murdered by your current lover, not your ex." His eyes narrowed at me in mock-anger.

"My apologies," I began sarcastically, looking out the window for a few beats. "I guess I'm not used to it yet," I whispered.

I heard Zack sigh from the driver's side. "Granted, it's

been a whirlwind."

"A whirlwind plus a decade."

Zack pursed his lips, eyes focused on the road, trying not to bite back.

We sat in comfortable silence as we watched the busy streets of London fade. It felt weird being out in the real world with Zack. We had been in the warm cocoon of the city, safe and sound, but now we were leaving our bubble, with only each other for company.

"I wouldn't take back that decade, though. If it didn't happen, I wouldn't be sitting in this car with you now. I wouldn't have been good enough for you. I barely am now, as it is, but I would be damned to have ruined your life any more than I already did. That decade led us here, and that seems worth it to me."

My mouth opened, taken aback by his words.

I nodded, unable to gather the words I needed to reply.

Was he right?

Maybe if we had been together all of these years, we wouldn't be as blissfully happy as we are now. Maybe the deep purple bruise he had left on my heart had been needed so that it could beat for him now. Maybe we just needed time to grow up and figure out all our shit.

We had been on the road for almost two hours when we pulled into a small village. Zack drove down a back road that neighboured bright green fields, heading towards a row of old stone cottages with thatched roofs.

We approached a small cottage, sunflowers towered either

side of the driveway leading to a duck egg blue front door. Zack pulled the car to a stop in front of the cottage.

"Holy shit," I muttered in disbelief. "Do you like it?" he asked, biting his lip.

"I love it! How did you even find a place like this so last minute?"

"There was a cancellation,"

"It must have cost a fortune." I got out of the car and began taking in the beauty of my surroundings. "You need to let me pay my half," I continued as he followed me towards the front door.

"Absolutely not. This is my treat, Lou." he walked towards me and kissed me on the temple. Warmth filled my body as his lips made contact with me. "We've got to celebrate you finishing your book!" He reached for the key box and entered the code to open it.

"It's not even been published yet," I chuckled.

"But it will be soon. I have every faith." He put the key into the old brass lock and opened the front door.

The door led straight into the kitchen. A table filled the centre of the room, with a large vase filled with sunflowers on top.

The wood cabinets were painted duck egg to match the front door, and the floors look like they were original natural wood of the house. At the back of the kitchen, there was a large window behind the farmhouse sink, the sun beamed through and showered the kitchen with beautiful countryside that was surrounding us.

"Did you plan all these sunflowers?" I raised my brows.

"No, but let's pretend I did." He winked.

"You planned all this? You are soooo romantic!" I squealed theatrically, teasing him.

Zack chuckled as he came up behind me and effortlessly scooped me up into his arms. I giggled and swung my arms around his neck for support.

"Shall we go and look at the bedroom?" He glanced down at me, meeting my gaze with a fierce intensity. "I hear it's really nice up there, and the bed looked really comfy in the pictures."

"Well, then I guess we need to go try it out then, don't we?"

Louise 2014

The bright white envelope with my address written in swirling black calligraphy looked up at me from the battered welcome mat. I'd been waiting for this to arrive for the last week.

I ran up the stairs, back into my room, and closed the door behind me, practically jumping on the bed with excitement. I turned the envelope over and carefully opened the flap, trying not to tear anything, pulling out the card from inside. It had *A & M* on the front in rose gold foil, surrounded by a circle of watercolour eucalyptus.

You are invited to the wedding of

Maeve Winter

&

Alexander Kennedy

On

Saturday 26th July 2014

The reality of Maeve getting married hit me at that moment, and a single tear fell down my cheek.

I was so happy for her, she was only twenty-one, but once Maeve set her mind to something, no one could change it— like when she dropped out of uni three months after starting, and moved from Leeds to London.

In true Maeve fashion, she dropped out with no plan, but pretty quickly found an internship at a PR firm for the following summer.

Her parents had been worried at first, but she was a natural at it. Of course, Alex had moved with her and worked as a chef in a restaurant near to where they lived.

Maeve was definitely enjoying the PR girl life a bit too much, and was always at fancy parties doing God knows what, but she was young, and they were happy in their little bubble.

It was no surprise when Alex popped the question the following year. It was also no surprise when Maeve decided she wanted to pull the wedding off in just six months.

I had spent many a night with her the last few weeks, planning, and this invitation was the first tangible item to show off all of our hard work.

I pulled my phone out of my pocket, opened the front camera, held the invite up to my face with a big smile, and clicked the button to take the picture.

I sent the picture to Maeve with the following message:

It's here! Xx

My phone rang moments later. I laughed at her eagerness and answered.

"Hey,"

"Do they look as good as you thought Lou?" Her voice was full of excitement.

"They're even more beautiful in person." It was true, they really were.

"Oh, thank God, I have been so worried. Anyway, I'll see you tomorrow for the dress fitting, right?"

"Yes, shall I just meet you there?"

"Yeah, I have to go get Mum from the station, so I may as well just catch you at the shop."

"Sounds perfect. Anyway, I better go, I need to get to my creative writing lecture."

"Yawn! I don't miss those. Enjoy! See you tomorrow at eleven, can't wait!" She hung up before I could respond.

It was February, I was in my second year and uni had just begun again. I went home for a couple of days over Christmas to see Dad and Faye, but I came back to the city for the rest of the winter break.

Since moving to London just over a year ago, I haven't been able to bear going home for longer than a few days at a time.

My last few months of living there had been so dark and lonely.

The fear I used to have about leaving, and missing home and the memories of Mum, had been replaced with a new-found desperation to never step foot in that town again.

I never wanted to relive the memories that I had made that last summer with Zack.

Starting my new life had helped me move on from what happened. I still thought about him when I saw something on Instagram or Facebook, or if I looked at my tattoo for too long, but it was more bearable from my student digs in London.

Alex and Maeve still saw Zack when he came to visit, and they spoke on the phone a lot.

Occasionally, I would hear his voice from the other end of the phone when I was at their flat, or sometimes they'd mention him in passing without thinking. They tried their best to hide it from me over the years, but that got harder and harder as time moved on and they couldn't hide their close friendship.

I just smiled and nodded if ever they spoke about him. There had been a few close run ins where he and Grace had arrived at their flat moments after I had left. But, luckily, I had gone the last year and a half avoiding seeing him—unless I gave into the urge to check his social media, which had become much less frequent as time had gone on.

I sighed aloud. Unfortunately, I wasn't going to be able to avoid them for much longer. In addition to Maeve making me her

Maid of Honour, Alex had made Zack his Best Man. It was only a matter of time before I was going to have to face him again—not to mention Grace.

The thought alone made me feel sick to my stomach.

I slotted the invite into the frame of my floor-length gold mirror.

*

I woke up before my alarm, feeling smug for missing the unbearable sound of the clock. Uni had dragged the day before, so maybe it would've been better to have stayed chatting on the phone to Maeve instead of attending. It was a lecture on contextual analysis, and it was always a drag on a Friday afternoon.

I had barely slept all last night. There was too much anticipation to see Maeve trying on potential wedding dresses.

It was going to be a day we would remember for the rest of our lives.

It was almost silent. No one else in the house was awake, they'd all been out drinking the night before at some terrible night club in Clapham that I refuse to go to, and they probably wouldn't get out of bed until late afternoon.

In all honesty, I didn't overly enjoy or participate in the university lifestyle, so I didn't have much to do with the three other girls that I lived with, but they were nice enough.

I had a few hours till I needed to leave, so I decided to take the rare opportunity for peace and quiet to write.

I opened up my laptop and opened up the document titled '*The Midnight Circle*'.

I had finished the first draft of the book during my *dark period*—as I called it—before uni, but I had slowly been editing it over the last year and a half. There really wasn't much more I felt I could add to it, I knew it was okay, but I wasn't convinced it was good enough to do anything with.

I doubted anyone would want to even read my query letter, let alone publish it, so I was just adding things that I had learned from uni to make it passable.

I put my phone on silent, set an alarm for ten, and entered my other world, letting the words flow through me and onto the page.

My alarm pinged, and I came back to reality. I'd made good headway, even coming up with an additional chapter idea. I glanced at my phone and saw three messages waiting for me.

One was from one of my housemates asking if I'd leave her a key as she'd lost hers the night before. The second was from Maeve:

Just on the way to meet mum! Don't forget your bridesmaid shoes!

The next message was from Dad:

Enjoy today love. Take lots of pics and ring me later! Dad.

He had been fully invested in the wedding since I told him the news. He loved Maeve so much and thought of her as another daughter. I think he thought this was his chance to see at least one of us get married.

I went to the bathroom and made myself sick, desperate to get the lunch I had earlier out of my body. It had become second nature at this point, part of my routine. Binging, purging, binging, purging. A never ending cycle.

I knew I needed to do it if I was going to have to look at myself in a mirror all afternoon in dresses.

I got in the shower and washed off any vomit that had gone onto my chin, letting the warm water replace the chill of the house.

I resented the feeling of the cold as I turned off the shower, and quickly wrapped up in a warm towel before brushing my hair into a low ponytail. I put on some mascara and concealer and flicked through my wardrobe to find as many layers as possible to keep me warm for my journey.

Once I had piled on some clothes, I grabbed the large shopper with my bridesmaid shoes in and headed for the door.

As I walked down the stairs, the smell of alcohol from the night before hit me like a train. I tried not to gag at the stench.

I got to the shop just before eleven. I waited outside for Maeve and her mum. The shop was beautiful; it was an old building in Marylebone. Windows were either side of the door, where the mannequins were dressed in the most beautiful dresses I had ever seen.

"Lou!" I turned around to see Maeve walking towards me. She'd done her hair in a half updo and her makeup mirrored how I know she wanted it for the wedding.

Her mum followed behind her; facially, they looked incredibly similar, except Jane had fake tanned skin and long blonde hair. She had a very intimidating presence, and was always dressed glamorously. I had never seen her without her heels on, even in their house.

I loved her so much.

I had known her my whole life, and despite coming across like a very scary woman on the surface, she had always been so tender with me. She had been best friends with Mum since they were in their twenties, and I guess she sort of stepped in as my mother figure when she died.

"Louise, darling." She pulled me in for a hug and kissed both my cheeks. "You look gorgeous."

"It's so good to see you," I replied.

Jane smiled, and held me by the shoulders, taking me in. "Right, come on then, girls," she said and ushered us into the shop.

The assistants took our things and poured us champagne. We trailed through the dresses in the shop, handing ones that we wanted to try to the shop assistant.

I knew this would go one of two ways. It would either be super hard or super easy. There was going to be absolutely no in between. Maeve and her mum knew exactly what they wanted and wouldn't settle for anything less.

Jane and I watched as Maeve came out in dress after dress, a blur of white and ivory lace. She looked phenomenal in everything she tried on, but we all knew we would know when she was in '*the one*'.

As Maeve was trying on what must have been her fiftieth dress, Jane turned to me and filled up my champagne glass.

"Are you enjoying your university course, darling?"

"Yeah, for the most part, it's really interesting. I'm learning a lot. I don't love the uni lifestyle as much but not long left."

She nodded. "You've never been one for that though, have you?" She smiled. "Your mum was the same way."

I felt my cheeks heat. I always felt uncomfortable when people compared me to Mum.

"Your dad seems to be doing well, so does Faye; she's got out of that mean teenager phase now," she joked. "Although, she's still a firecracker."

"Yeah, she actually wants to talk to me these days. It's nice."

"You should see them more. They miss you," she said. I knew she wasn't digging at me; she was being honest. They did miss me, and I missed them. I just found being there so hard.

I just nodded in agreement, not wanting to go into it.

Maeve walked out in a princess style dress, strapless with a full body skirt of tulle. It was beautiful, but way too much. We all looked at each other and shook our heads. Maeve turned back into the dressing room.

"I met Zack's girlfriend." Jane said quietly

My heart sank at the sound of his name. I wasn't sure what Jane knew but knowing how close she and Maeve were, I assumed she knew everything.

"Oh yeah?" I asked.

"Not a patch on you, kid. She's stuck up and he doesn't have an opinion of his own anymore. You've made a lucky escape if you ask me."

My lips twitched into a smile.

Maeve walked out of the dressing room again.

Time stopped.

She was wearing a fishtail ivory Carmeuse gown that hugged her curves effortlessly. It looked like it had been made just for her.

She had a plain veil that stopped around her hips and slotted into her hair. I turned to see Jane crying, and my eyes filled up instantly.

I turned back towards Maeve.

"This is the one," she said softly.

I nodded in agreement as Jane stood up and hugged her daughter. I cried a little bit more, realising I would never have this moment. My Mum would never get to see me in a wedding dress, getting married, having children.

"Right then." Jane stepped back, regaining her composure. "We will take this one, please," she said to the assistant, who quickly took measurements.

Once Maeve was ready and back in her clothes, Jane turned to me. “Come on then Lulu, get your bottom in there, and we will hand you some dresses.”

Maeve rolled her eyes at her Mum before she smirked at me. “You will look beautiful, don’t worry.” She ushered me into the changing room, and I began taking off my layers.

“Don’t go in there. I’ll take them in,” I heard Maeve shout. I assumed she was talking to the shop assistant, knowing full well I’d die on the spot if a stranger saw me getting undressed.

Maeve pulled the curtain open just enough to put her hand through, passing me over a satin sage green dress. “Trust me,” she whispered.

I grimaced as I took the dress from her.

I pulled on the dress and took a deep breath, bracing myself as I walked out of the changing room.

I saw the colour leave Jane's face when she saw me. Maeve looked at me open-mouthed, and if I didn’t know any better, I’d say she was trying not to cry. Did I really look that bad?

I stood there, unsure what to do next. Jane stood up and smiled.

“Well, what a lovely colour that is on you.” She walked towards me and adjusted the dress. “Nothing a bit of tailoring can’t fix,”

I smiled unsure, I looked down and realised the dress was drowning me, how thin was I? I glanced over at Maeve, she avoided eye contact with me as she attempted a quivering smile. I smiled back at her reassuringly.

It wasn't her fault she hadn't noticed. She never saw me in skimpy clothes, and she'd been so busy with the wedding recently. She had bigger things going on.

I went back into the changing room and put my clothes back on, trying not to look at myself in the mirror anymore.

I handed the dress to the shop assistant, and we made our way over to the till to place our dress orders. Jane insisted she paid for mine too, which I was grateful for as it would have taken me months to pay it off.

"How about some lunch?" she said as we left the shop.

*

I checked my phone later that night and saw a voicemail from Jane.

"I'm so sorry you've got to this point without anyone noticing how bad things were. Maeve will be ridden with guilt, and so am I. I know things have been hard for you since your mum, but she would hate to know how it's been affecting you. I won't mention things to your Dad but I'm getting you help, no negotiation. I have the name of a therapist for you, I can set up the meeting, and I'll pay for it all. It can be our secret. Not even Maeve needs to know if that's what you want. Get in touch. I love you, Lulu."

I listened to her words on repeat whilst burying my head into my pillow and crying until I eventually fell asleep.

Louise Present Day

"Good morning." I turned over, my eyes adjusting to the light pouring into the room. Zack sat up in bed, and looked down at me curiously.

"Why are you looking at me like that?" I asked croakily, my mouth dry.

"You snore, did you know that?" His eyes were glinted with humour.

"Shut up. No, I don't." I pulled a pillow from under my head and threw it at his head.

"You absolutely do. You sound like a warthog," he laughed.

I grumbled loudly, turning my back away from him in protest.

"It's cute." He began tickling my ribs. I kicked him and squealed. "I might have to keep that secret, though, I'm not sure everyone else would agree with me."

"Oh, yeah?" I said curiously.

"Yeah, I'll add it to the sack I keep right up here," he said, tapping his head.

My mind flashed back through the catalogue of secrets that had ruined out relationship. My body stiffened, and he let go. I began getting out of bed and reaching for the white waffle dressing gown draped over the radiator. His words 'secret' began replaying in my head. I knew he hadn't meant anything by it, but the idea of having any more secrets was too much to comprehend.

"Are you okay?" he asked.

"Yeah. I just want a shower." I smiled back at him half-heartedly and walked into the ensuite.

I grabbed my toothbrush and put the toothpaste on the bristles. and began aggressively brushing my teeth, trying to remain as rational as possible.

He had been nothing but honest about his commitment this time, and I shouldn't let the past affect our present. But I couldn't shake that fact that I hadn't met his friends or family—I barely even knew their names—and he hadn't said I love you yet.

Although, it had only been a few weeks. People in relationships wait months before any of that. Perhaps it was easier to treat this as totally fresh, a new relationship.

"Lou?" I heard a soft tap on the door before it opened.

Zack's face popped around the door. "Please don't just pretend everything is fine if it's not. Talk to me."

"I'm just being silly, don't worry about it," I said quietly as I spat my toothpaste into the sink.

"Lou, I know communication isn't our strong point, but I can't help if you don't tell me what's wrong." He was fully in the room at this point, watching me with intent.

I sighed heavily. "I've just always felt like your secret. You've always kept your feelings for me to yourself, and, truthfully, I've never felt like you'd be proud to be with me." He looked broken, but I kept going, "Grace got to be with you publicly. Minus Alex and Maeve, who else has ever known about us?" I sighed. "I'm trying, I am, to forget the past, but it's still early days, and some things might just take me some time."

He kept staring at me, the water in his eyes reflecting in the light from the window, his mouth slightly open as if figuring out what to say. I fidgeted, suddenly very uncomfortable with my vulnerability.

"I'm going to go on a walk. I'll be back in a bit." He left the bathroom, and I heard the front door slam shut only moments later.

I stood, frozen, toothpaste from the brush dripping onto the floor.

What had I done? How had I ruined this already?

Tears began to form, falling down my cheeks. I felt my stomach convulse, and I wretched, supporting myself on the sink.

Pain twisted in my stomach from trying to throw up with no food in my body.

I took several deep breaths, and suddenly my sadness turned into anger.

How dare he walk out on me? How dare he make me question how I feel?

I washed my face and began getting ready, feeling numb and trying not to let him get to me. If I stopped to think about him leaving me again, I'd collapse.

Two hours passed, and I heard nothing. My anger was increasing minute by minute, overruling any worries I had about losing him. I was sitting outside in the back garden, letting the sun blaze my skin as I scrim read my book, trying to distract myself, when I heard footsteps from within the house.

I didn't move. There was no way I was going to him first.

I could hear the sound of cabinets opening and closing and pots and pans clanging. Was this guy seriously making himself something to eat right now?

After what felt like forever, I heard him calling my name to come inside. I stood up reluctantly, pulled the straps of my top up, and made my way inside.

"Hi." He was standing on the other end of the kitchen arms behind his back.

The table had been set for two, and two plates were filled with steak, chips and a bright green salad, accompanied by two glasses of white wine. The smell worked its way into my nostrils.

"Before you shout at me, can you please let me talk?"

He could sense my anger; the tension in my body, the furrowed brow on my face and the hands on my hips.

"I know I've fucked up. I know you are mad." His hands were held up in surrender. "I left, not because I was mad at you, but because I was mad at myself. I think the reality of how poorly I've treated you over the years just hit me, and I had to leave to clear my head."

"You don't walk out and go missing for two hours and not tell me why or where you're going. We're fucking grown ups."

"I know, you're right. I just panicked. I've only ever been with one other person, and when we would fight, it was just better to leave. I shouldn't have assumed you would act the same." He looked down at the floor. "I just don't want you to ever be upset with me. I don't want to lose you again."

I remained silent, letting my anger settle.

"I never meant to make you feel like a secret, Lou. But, it's true, you have been my secret for almost ten years. Ever since that summer, my feelings for you have been buried inside me, and I've had to keep it a secret, us a secret. But you aren't a secret anymore, Lou. We aren't a secret anymore. I want everyone to know we're together."

I could feel my heart softening as he spoke.

"I may have overreacted, but my feelings are valid," I said.

"Of course, they're valid. You have every right to feel that way." He took a few steps toward me. "I'm sorry, Lou." He paused before coming any closer, using his eyes to seek permission.

I nodded, and he closed the gap between us. My breath quickened as I felt his presence overpower mine. He wrapped me tightly in his arms, and my body relaxed into him.

"It's okay," I whispered, nuzzling myself into his chest.

He kissed the top of my head and then pulled away, "Come on, we need to eat this before it gets cold."

I sat at the table and sipped my wine. "It looks amazing."

"Well, Alex taught me this recipe, so if it's inedible, blame him."

"Yeah, nothing to do with the chef at all," I laughed. Zack kicked me under the table.

I picked up my glass and raised it towards him, "To us."

"To us."

Louise 2014

I had spent the last few months leading up to the wedding trying to get better. My therapy had started the week after Jane had texted me. Surprisingly it was working.

Don't get me wrong, it wasn't an easy process. Therapy was tiring… and exhausting. I'd had a few wobbles since beginning the sessions, but with the help of my counsellor and Jane, progress had definitely been made and I'd managed to somewhat stay on track.

Maeve had been keeping an eye on me too. I knew she had felt guilty that day in the bridal shop. She had broken down crying to me, saying how sorry she was a few days later.

The wedding was only a week away now, and between uni deadlines and helping organise everything for the big day, it had been non-stop. I handed in my final assignment last week, and part of me was dreading the long summer without the routine of uni to distract myself. I decided the best option was to go full time at the coffee shop over the summer in an attempt to keep myself occupied.

It was just past nine in the morning, and I was meeting Maeve before we got the train back home together, to get everything ready and where it needed to be.

It was a hot day, too hot. I hoped for her sake it would cool down a bit for the wedding next week.

I worked my way through Kings Cross, heading straight to get us both a coffee for the train home. I ordered two lattes and sat on the chairs outside the shop, waiting for Maeve.

Ten minutes later, I noticed her clambering towards me, carrying enough luggage for a two week holiday. She had large black sunglasses on and her curls thrown into some sort of pile on top of her head.

She nodded in acknowledgement as she approached me "Hey," she croaked.

"Hey, you okay?" I asked.

She took off her sunglasses and took a seat. She looked awful.

Her eyes were bloodshot, her bags deep and dark, and her skin was breaking out. Maeve had never looked bad a day in her life, but this was becoming more and more common these days. I was sure it was just the stress of the wedding.

"I had a work event last night, got in about three hours

ago. I haven't managed to sleep yet," she groaned between sips of her latte. This also wasn't uncommon for Maeve recently. Bar checking in on therapy now and then, she was pretty unreachable, especially in the evening when she was out enjoying the party scene.

"When's Alex coming down?" I asked to change the subject.

"He's coming down tomorrow. He couldn't get work off today," she grumbled.

We grabbed our bags and headed to the platform to board the train. It was only an hour train, thank God. Maeve slept most of the way, not managing much more than small talk through the journey.

I scanned over the query letter I had written for my book. There was nothing more I could do. The possibility of someone wanting to be my agent and represent me was unlikely, but it didn't stop me. That was a lesson I'd be uncomfortably learning from therapy, my weight does not define my success, and slowly it was starting to infiltrate the darker thoughts.

The hunt for literary agents had been endless, I'd been looking for Young Adult fantasy, and had narrowed it down to an initial fifteen. I had meticulously written a personalised letter to each one. I typed in their names on my emails one by one and hit send. At least if I sent them now, I wouldn't have time to obsess over unanswered emails—not until I was back in London, anyway.

The train drew closer to our destination, and I watched the familiar surroundings appear in the window; the buildings I had been in, the park I had played at, the people I had known. Something that should be peaceful, nostalgic but instead made my heart race and my palms moist. The bad memories creeping in.

As the train pulled in, the anxiety bubbled up from my feet up towards my stomach. I could see Dad eagerly waiting at the station for us. He was waving frantically with a huge smile on his face. I hadn't seen him since Christmas. I was avoiding him. The last thing he needed was to be worrying about me even more than normal.

We headed off the train. Dad came towards us and gave us both a hug before taking our bags.

"Hey girls, it's lovely to see you both. How was your journey?"

"It was fine, thanks, Dave. How are you?" Maeve had regained some energy. She would never want to come across as rude to anyone, especially to my dad. They had a soft spot for each other.

"Is Faye home?" I asked after we dropped Maeve home.

"Probably not, love, she'll be out gallivanting somewhere."

Faye was enjoying her summer before her last year of school, and I couldn't blame her for wanting to be out all the time. She was a lot more social than me.

"So, love, I've been meaning to tell you something." He gripped the steering wheel tightly as his eyes focused on the road.

"What?" *Had he spoken to Jane?*

He coughed. "I—uh—I've met someone," he blurted out.

My heart sank. My eyes stung. I could feel the tears coming.

How could he do this? How could he do this to mum?

"Okay," I whispered.

"Please don't cry, Lou. I know it's hard." He paused. "She's not your mum, and she never will be, but she makes me happy. I've not felt this happy in years." He glanced at me, weighing up whether I would respond. "Please just meet her?"

I felt bad. The crying was an automatic response. It was hard to imagine how he could ever be in love with someone who wasn't Mum, but I knew it was unfair of me.

"No, Dad, I'm sorry. If you're happy, that's all that matters. I just need a little time, that's all." I was lying but I knew it was wrong for me to burden him with that.

"I know, love. Take all the time you need." He smiled at me softly as a tear formed in his eye. He looked back at the road, thinking I hadn't noticed.

"What's her name?"

"Vicki."

We arrived home a few minutes later. Dad got my bags out

of the car, and I headed to open the door. I immediately noticed the change of atmosphere as I stepped into the house.

The smell of cotton hit me, and it was spotless.

I looked through the rooms downstairs, where there were now candles and throws, cushions and flowers on the window ledge. I didn't really know what to think. There was a part of me that was happy for my dad, happy that he was healing and moving on. But there was also a lump lodged in my throat the size of a tennis ball.

I missed Mum. I wished she were here. I wished she were the one making my dad happy. I wished she were the one causing him to go out and buy ridiculous cotton and Bergamot scented candles to make the house feel more like home.

But she was gone.

I threw my bags over my shoulder and walked up to my bedroom.

Unlike the rest of the house, nothing had changed.

It was the same as it had always been. The same pink wallpaper I'd had since I was fourteen was staring at back at me. The same pictures of Maeve, Mum and me hung in their frames, all dotted around the room. Stacks of books I had read years ago were piled high on my desk, surrounded by old battered notepads that were full of plans for my own novel.

I flopped on my bed and looked up at the ceiling. I hated this room. I hated who I was when I lived here, especially

who I was in those last few months. I had stared at this same ceiling for hours on end, coming up with endless ways I wasn't good enough, and wallowing in the misery of heartbreak.
I didn't want to do that anymore.

It was early afternoon, and I couldn't bear the thought of sitting in my room all week, reliving the past.

I got a sudden burst of energy.

It was time for a fresh start.

I began sorting through my room, placing old belongings into *keep* or *throw* piles, digging through every single item that had been hoarded; things I hadn't seen since I was a child, clothes I hadn't worn in a decade.

The bin bags filled a corner of my room. Dad had gone out to get me some paint, thrilled I finally wanted to make my bedroom my own again. I guessed he thought that if I liked my room, I might've actually wanted to come home more often.

The last step was to clean out my bedside table.

I rifled through the drawers, throwing all the random junk away. I noticed a folded up piece of paper in the back corner of one of the drawers. I opened it up and gasped.

It was me. The drawing of me Zack had given me all those years before.

Tears rolled down my eyes and onto the paper.

I forgot how much I loved this picture. I looked so beautiful and happy.

The memory of her, and that version of me, had all but

faded, she had been stolen from me. Zack had seen her, he'd helped her see her own light. But just as quickly, he'd ripped it all away.

I hated him for that.

I folded the drawing back up and put it in my desk drawer. I didn't want to throw it away, I needed it as a reminder of who I was and who I would one day be again.

*

The week at home flew by, and I had finished decorating my room. I painted the walls a forest green and varnished all my furniture to darker wood.

They may have just been surface-level changes, but it was the fresh start I needed, my home felt like home again.

I'd gotten used to the changes around the house too. I guess you could say I was adjusting to the idea of a woman in my dad's life again. A woman who wasn't Mum.

I'd forced myself to get used to it, asking him questions every now and again about Vicki. It
was hard to ignore the glint in my dad's eyes just talking about her. So I knew it was time to grow up and face reality. To meet the woman who has my dad smiling and whistling around the house again.

It was just a few days before the wedding, and Vicki was coming over for dinner. I was nervous, nervous I wouldn't like her, nervous she wouldn't like me, nervous it would bring back feelings about Mum that I didn't want to think about.

I went downstairs to greet her once I heard the doorbell chime. She was a curvy brunette woman in her late forties, and her energy was warm and friendly. She wasn't so bad, I supposed.

As we ate dinner, she told us all about her life. She had been divorced for six years, had no children of her own and was a teacher at a high school.

In turn, she asked me questions about my book and my life, seeming genuinely interested. She was lovely, and Dad had been smiling the whole time she was there. Even Faye seemed to like her.

Maybe our family was finally starting to heal.

Louise Present Day

The rest of our trip was heaven. We'd spent our days walking in the countryside, appreciating the fresh air, and our evenings relaxing in the hot tub.

The weeks since the trip were spent in a bubble of love, sex and food, seeing each other almost every night now we had a taste for it. The days had even been filled with some freelance writing.

Kayleigh rang to ask when I was returning to the real world again, and I promised I would go for dinner with her next week.

But I couldn't deny I was living in ecstasy.

I finally had the man that I had always loved, love *me* back. I was the girl in the drawing again.

She was home.

I kept telling myself that I wasn't living with my head in

the clouds, that it was all real.

Zack and I were meeting Alex after work. I looked out of my window and admired the view. It was my favourite time in London.

Autumn was starting to creep in, the leaves on the trees outside were beginning to brown, and the air had a slight chill.

As I looked outside, I mulled over my feelings about seeing Alex. I was nervous. It was always awkward when we caught up, full of small talk and awkward silences.

I wasn't sure how much he knew about Zack and me, but I was glad I had him as a buffer.

Zack arrived at my flat early in the evening. He was wearing a black shirt with black jeans and converse, and he smelt like fresh aftershave.

"You look handsome," I said, kissing him hard from missing him all day.

"As do you." He spun me around the lounge, taking me all in.

I was wearing a black t-shirt dress, a plaid shirt and Dr Martens. It was a simple look, but I knew it was just how he liked me.

He pulled me close, securing me with his hands on the small of my back, placing a kiss on the side of my neck. "Are you ready to go?" he whispered, moving his kiss onto my cheek.

I took a deep breath. "Ready as I'll ever be."

Zack pulled away and looked at me. "Don't be nervous.

He's looking forward to seeing you."

I'd slightly touched on the Maeve subject with Zack over the last few nights, but I knew he would never fully understand what Alex and I had been through together.

Mine and Alex's relationship was now a tie we couldn't break, but one that neither of us wanted to be a part of.

We left the flat and made our way to the tube station. We arrived at the bar in Camden around half an hour later.

It was cooler outside than expected, so Zack gave me his jacket to keep me warm. We headed to the back of the bar and sat on the same side of a booth whilst we waited for Alex.

I kept my arms wrapped around my body and ordered a double vodka and lemonade. Zack laughed as I guzzled it the moment the waitress put it down on the table.

Alex arrived not long after we did. He looked well. The colour had returned to his face, his bags had gone, and he'd shaved. As he got closer, I could see the light in his eyes had somewhat returned.

I hadn't seen him like this for a long time, and I couldn't help but smile when I saw how he looked… *whole* again.

"Lou, it's so good to see you." Alex pulled me in for a hug.

He was so tall I could only manage to put my arms around his waist.

"You look really good, Alex," I said, grabbing his arms and taking him all in. I took my seat whilst Alex and Zack greeted each other.

Once Zack took his seat again, he squeezed my thigh under the table.

"Well, I'm not going to lie, it's about fucking time you two got together." Alex smirked.

I laughed and rolled my eyes.

"Yeah, well, I'll take responsibility for that taking so long." Zack looked down at his pint glass, awkwardly shaking his head as heat flushed his face.

"Maeve would have loved this," Alex said, locking eyes with me, smiling gently.

My heart twinged at the sound of her name. I knew we couldn't ignore the elephant in the room all evening, but I hadn't anticipated her coming up five minutes into his arrival.

I smiled back at him. "Actually, I think she would have probably told Zack he's a dickhead and threatened him not to hurt me again."

Both Alex and Zack laughed in unison.

"Yeah, you're right there." Alex beamed, but I could see a glimpse of pain in his eyes.

We ordered some more drinks and I sat back and listened to Zack tell the story of how we ended up back in each other's lives again.

"Sounds like fate to me." Alex grinned.

Zack turned around to face me and smiled. "I think so."

"So, are you still at the restaurant you mentioned last time we spoke?" I asked, turning the conversation away from us.

"Yes, although I do have some news," he said, clearing his throat.

"Go on," Zack probed.

"Well, I'm opening my own restaurant. It's gunna have a bar too."

"Oh my god, what?" I shot up in my seat. "Where?"

"Back in Brixton. It used to be a café, just got the go ahead to renovate it. I'm gunna have a street-food style menu and maybe themed weeks with guest chefs and some live music." His eyes twinkled as he talked.

"Oh, Alex. It sounds amazing. I'm so happy for you!" I beamed, my heart full of pride.

"Yeah. You deserve it, mate, you really do," Zack added.

"Thanks." Alex paused, looking between us. "I'm selling the flat to help pay for the renovations."

I nodded without saying anything. I couldn't object. He had every right to sell it.

He couldn't be expected to stay in that flat forever, especially after everything that happened. I could barely step foot in there myself.

"I think that's a great idea," I finally replied, not knowing what else to say.

"Do you want to come over before I move? There's some

of your stuff still there. You might want some of it?" He hesitated.

"I'd like that." I wasn't sure I *would* like that. That flat haunted me. But there were some things there that I knew I wanted, and maybe it was necessary for me to finally draw a line under that part of my life.

We didn't bring her up again for the rest of the night. We drank and drank and didn't stop laughing, Alex had always been the life and soul of the party, and it was lovely to see him be his old self again.

Just before midnight, we decided to call it a night.

"I'll go sort the bill," Zack offered.

"Are you sure, mate?"

"Yeah, you'll be giving me free food for life now. It's the least I can do," Zack joked before walking towards the bar. Alex and I strolled to the front door.

"It's really good to see you happy again," I said, nudging Alex's shoulder.

"Same. Think it's about time we got to be happy again." He put his arm around me. After a moment of silence, he turned to face me. "Lou—" he paused. "I don't want to overstep here, but I think Maeve would have wanted me to say it."

I looked up at him, confused.

"I don't want to overstep here but you need to be careful with Zack. Please don't let him hurt you again, okay?"

I was taken aback. Zack was his best friend. Why would

he say that? Before I could reply, Zack came out to meet us in the street.

"Ready?" he asked.

I nodded before looking back at Alex. He looked at me with wide eyes, silently begging for me not to say anything.

Zack held out his hand for me. I grabbed it and began walking. The breeze was even cooler now and had picked up its pace, it stung my cheeks as it hit my skin.

"Not as bad as you thought, huh?" Zack asked, stroking my hand with his thumb.

"No, not at all, it was really fun." I kept my eyes on where I was walking, I couldn't stop thinking about what Alex had just said, and I knew Zack would be able to read me like a book if I looked at him for too long.

"How do you feel about him selling the flat?"

"I don't know, we had a lot of good times there, but the bad memories outweigh them. I think it's time we all finally move on."

"Yeah, I think so. I can come to help you both, I don't mind," he offered. He was being so sweet. How could Alex think his intentions weren't genuine?

"I'm sure Alex and I can get through most of it, but maybe come when we're done, to say goodbye to the place?"

It wasn't fair to keep him away, he'd spent a lot of time at the flat, too, but I wanted my chance to be alone with Alex to get the answers I needed. Was it just the past, or did he know something I didn't?

When we got into bed that night, Zack began to kiss me. I knew what he wanted, and normally, I would want it too, but I couldn't shake it off.

"I'm tired, I'm sorry," I murmured.

"That's okay, babe. Night." He kissed me softly on the nose, and I turned my back to him.

I kept my eyes open and stared out the window. All the memories of the pain he'd put me through were replaying in my head. Was I being stupid?

Louise 2014

I had spent the rest of the week leading up to the wedding with Alex and Maeve, making centrepieces, threading bunting and checking the favours had been done to perfection.

Alex and I were exhausted. Maeve was in full bridezilla mode and had us following very strict orders.

It was Thursday morning, two days before the wedding. I was reading in bed, enjoying the peace and quiet before another day of wedding stress began when my phone rang.

"So, I have some news," Maeve greeted me when I answered.

"Oh God, what? Are you pregnant?!"

"God no!" she shouted "Erm, so Zack's arriving today."

"Well, shit." My heart sank. I knew I had to see him at the

wedding, but I'd hoped the crowd would mean I could avoid him as much as possible. My brain hadn't anticipated a pre-wedding encounter. I was not mentally prepared.

"Yeah. I've sent him and Alex off to go and run some errands, so hopefully you can avoid him." She paused. "Grace isn't coming until the day though, so at least you won't have to see her."

God, I forgot I was going to have to see them together.

"Lou?"

"Sorry," I began, sighing. "Well, I'm going to have to see him at some point, aren't I? May as well rip the plaster off." I tried to sound convincing.

"Don't let him get to you, Lou. You're in such a good place. Don't let him knock your confidence. I'll see you in an hour?"

"Yeah, sure." I hung up the phone.

I knew what she was scared of, and I was scared of it too, the urge to binge and purge was already in the pit of my stomach, and I was fighting against every instinct I had.

It was around seven, and I'd managed to avoid Zack all day. Maeve kept sending him and Alex out for pointless things.

I wasn't sure how many of these errands were real, but I appreciated it all the same.

After working tirelessly all day, we decided to get some food. Maeve was not one of these brides who was worried about what she ate in the days leading up to her wedding. I swear, she'd never gained or lost more than five pounds in her life.

We were sitting at the large marble kitchen island Maeve's house when we heard the door go. We both looked at each other, knowing exactly who it was.

"You've got this," she mouthed at me.

"Hello, my lovely wife to be," Alex called as he made his way through to the kitchen.

"Is everything done?" She looked at him, unamused. "Yes, master." He saluted before pulling her in for a kiss.

Before I knew it, Zack entered the room. His hair was longer, his skin tanned, and his arms patchworked with tattoos. His presence filled the room.

He looked straight at me. Our eyes were locked, neither of us knowing how the other would react.

"Hi," he said softly.

"Hi," I replied, not letting any emotion show in my voice. I could feel Alex and Maeve darting their eyes between us, not knowing what to say or do.

"How are you?" he continued, standing still by the door, unsure if he was stepping into a war zone.

"Good, you?" I could tell my face and tone were unreadable, but I didn't care.

"Good, thanks." There was a long pause. Not the comfortable kind.

"Come get some food then, guys," Maeve's voice broke the tension.

We sat around the island, Zack and I on opposing sides.

Maeve and Alex did most of the talking, but I could feel Zack's
gaze burning me.

Once the last of the food had been eaten and the conversation had faded, I stood up from the stool and began collecting my things.

"I should head off. Thanks for the food. Maeve, I'll see you tomorrow." I hugged her tightly.

"Can't wait to spend my last night of freedom with you," Maeve joked, elbowing Alex playfully.

"I should go too," Zack said. He stood up and made his way towards me.

"Do you want a lift?" he asked once we stepped outside.

"No thanks, I drove." I replied.

"Okay." He was staring at the ground, as if he wanted to say a lot more than he was. "It's nice to see you again."

"You too. Bye." I turned and got into my car. I could feel him still standing there, watching me.

Rage built up in my body. Why couldn't he just leave me alone? What did he care? He was happy with Grace. He was only talking to me to clear his conscience, but it wasn't my job to make him feel less guilty.

Although, maybe this wasn't as excruciating for him. After all, he hadn't been the one who was humiliated and made to look like a fool with a crush she had mistaken for love.

I decided then that if I was going to get through this

weekend, I would have to be as civil as possible, if not for me, then for Alex and Maeve.

*

The wedding day was beautiful. The air was fresh, there the sun from blaring down too aggressively. Maeve, Jane and I had spent the night before cuddled up in Maeve's room, looking through old photos of us dressed up in bedsheets, pretending we were brides. We laughed over the boys that Maeve had dated over the years, and cried when Jane told us how her and my mum had gotten ready on the morning of their wedding days.

The morning had been calm and collected. The hair and makeup artists were blown away by the tranquillity in the room. There was no hesitation or cold feet; Maeve knew she was about to marry her soul mate, and so did the rest of us.

We all cried when her dad, Tony, saw her in her dress. She looked so classic, but still had her wild curls out to mirror her personality. We cried even more when Alex saw her walking down the aisle.

She took his breath away, rendering him utterly speechless.

They declared their vows to love each other for eternity.

Zack and I avoided eye contact throughout the whole ceremony. We took the pictures together, being as cordial as possible—arm-in-arm—not saying a word.

It hadn't been as bad as I thought. The love Maeve and Alex exuded was contagious, and more powerful than any feelings of negativity I was harbouring.

The reception was in a beautifully converted barn, decorated in peonies and eucalyptus. We had eaten a delicious meal, drank endless champagne, cried and laughed over the speeches. It had single-handedly become the best day of my life.

As the day was turning into the evening, and more guests began to arrive, Maeve and I snuck outside so she could smoke without her grandparents seeing. "Shit," she exclaimed.

"What?" I followed her eye line, confused until I saw her.

There she was.

Grace.

I had seen pictures of her, but she was even more beautiful in person. Her legs were twice as long as mine, perfectly tanned and adorned in floral tattoos. Her long brown hair flowed down her back to just above her hips, the caramel highlights glimmering in the golden hour sun.

She was wearing a black low cut strappy wrap dress, which cinched in at her waist, the straps tied up around her back which was also covered in tattoos. The skirt was split high and flowed around her legs as she walked.

"Ugh, who wears black to a wedding?" Maeve said as she stubbed out her cigarette. She could see the pain on my face and exhaled. "Look, she may be hot, but she's arrogant. Always has been. She thinks the sun shines out of her arse."

I laughed. "You don't need to humour me. He must like her for a reason."

"Whatever that reason is, I sure as hell can't put my finger on it. Come on. I should go back in."

We made our way back to the courtyard outside the barn, where Maeve began greeting a stream of evening guests who had appeared in our absence.

I took the opportunity to avoid any awkward run-ins and headed for the bathroom to freshen up. I looked in the mirror and topped up my lipstick.

I was interrupted by the toilet flushing, and then the cubicle door opened.

Fuck.

"Hi, you're Maeve's friend, right?" Grace said, tilting her head to the side. "Sorry, my mind has gone blank on your name."

Double fuck.

I hated her already.

"Erm, yeah. I'm Lou."

"Right." She looked me up and down and smiled at me disingenuously. "Do you know Zack then? I'm Grace, his girlfriend." I cringed as she spoke. She began washing her hands, keeping her eyes on herself in the mirror the whole time.

"Yeah. I know him a bit," I replied, unsure how much she knew.

She turned to get a paper towel and began drying her hands. She threw the towel in the bin and headed for the door.

"Well, see you around, Lou." She looked down at my wrist as she opened the door and said, "Cute tattoo," before she left.

I stood there for a moment, utterly perplexed at what had just happened.

Did she know about the tattoo?

Did she know I was lying? Did she really know my name?

I headed out of the bathroom and towards Maeve.

"You were right. Grace... she's…a lot," I whispered in Maeve's ear as I approached her.

I tried to put it behind me and danced the rest of the night away.

We had drunk so much throughout the day that I could barely keep track of how much I had consumed.

As the alcohol took over my body, I was suddenly overwhelmed by the heat of the room. My head began to spin. I saw the open barn doors and made a bee line for them. I needed air.

An old wooden bench was placed at the side of the courtyard, so I decided to take a breather away from the madness.

I closed my eyes and let my body fall into the seat. Smiling to myself, thinking about what a magical day it had been, how happy I was for Maeve.

A few moments later, I heard footsteps approaching. Whoever it was, was drunk by the sounds of their stumbling. I pulled my head up and opened my eyes.

"Louise Moore, how are ya?" Zack stood in front of me,

his body hunched and his voice cocky. Neither suited him.

"Your girlfriend is pleasant," I spat. The champagne had taken over my mouth.

"Ah, you met her, did you?" He took a seat next to me.

I edged to the side of the bench so that our bodies had as much distance between us as possible.

"Today was nice," he slurred.

"Yeah, it was. Perfect day for a perfect couple."

"Yeah. Must be nice," looking down at his hands.

"You have Grace," I snapped.

"It's not the same. We don't have that kind of love." He paused. "We used to be so close, Lou. What happened?"

"I'm sorry, did you forget what you did?" I couldn't believe the nerve of him. How dare he?

"I've only felt like I could have that kind of love with one other person before." He turned his head and looked at me. "We could have had it."

I shot up seeing red. "What is wrong with you?" I spat.

"Lou, I..." He tried to reach out for my hand, but I recoiled.

"You do *not* get to do this." I cross my arms in front of my chest. "You chose her. You don't get to go back on that just because you're drunk and bored. Especially not with me."

"Lou, please. It's not like that." He looked up at me, his eyes wide.

"You *broke* me." Tears streamed uncontrollably down my

face as my voice broke. "Go back to your girlfriend, Zack. She loves you." I turned away and ran back into the barn.

My vision blurred from the tears as I headed up to the room I was staying in, avoiding eye contact with everyone I passed.

Once I'd shut the door, I wiped my tears and checked my phone. It was just after midnight. I
guessed I could stay up here now. Everyone would think I just got too drunk and needed to go to bed. I couldn't go back down there and face him again. I couldn't stand there watching him pretend to be happy when he had just said all those things to me.

Was he really not happy, or was he just drunk?

Did he think we could have had the same love that Alex and Maeve did?

No, surely not, or he wouldn't have left me for Grace in the first place. And he would have reached out over the years.

He had made his choice then, and it was time I finally moved on.

Louise Present Day

"I'm bringing someone tonight that I want you to meet," Kayleigh said unexpectedly.

"Okay, what's his name?" She'd never wanted me to meet anyone she was dating before.

"It's Ada." She looked at me, waiting for my reaction. "That girl I went on a date with a few weeks ago."

"I'm more surprised that you want me to meet someone, not that she is a she," I laughed.

"Yeah, fair enough." She still didn't seem convinced.

"You've slept with girls before. What's the issue?" I asked.

"Yes, but I haven't dated one. It's a whole different ball game."

I smiled at her reassuringly. "Why didn't you tell me if it

was this serious?"

"Well, you've been slightly preoccupied with your own love life of late."

I grabbed her hand. "I'm sorry, I've been such a shitty friend."

"It's okay, you have every right to be a bit consumed at the moment."

"Tell me about her, please."

"She's a fashion buyer, she's twenty-nine, and she looks like a model."

"Show me a picture."

Kayleigh got out her phone and began swiping through several images of her and Ada on her phone.

She was right. She did look like a model.

She had piercing brown eyes, deep and rich skin, her hair braided and adorned. "Wow. She's beautiful," I gushed. "Have you slept with her yet?"

"I'm monogamous, Lou, not dead. Anyway, like I was saying, she's coming tonight, so it will be a double date. How grown-up of us."

"I've never been on a proper double date. I mean, Maeve and I used to hang out with Alex and Zack together, but nothing like this."

"We're basically signing ourselves up for marriage." She slid one of my rings off my index finger and onto my ring finger. "Will you marry me, Louise Moore?"

"Always." I winked.

She beamed, "Right, I need to go. I'll see you later." "See you tonight."

"I look forward to meeting the man himself," she said before leaving the flat.

I was not looking forward to it. I knew Kayleigh was protective, and she was also brash and honest, so it was inevitable she would interrogate Zack.

*

I arrived at the cocktail bar without Zack. He had said he was running late with work and would meet me there.

Kayleigh waved when she saw me. Ada was sitting with her—she was twice as beautiful in person.

I hugged Kayleigh when I approached the table.

"Lou, this is Ada," Kayleigh introduced us.

"It's lovely to meet you," I replied, smiling at Ada.

"You too, Kayleigh has told me so much about you."

All of a sudden, I felt guilty again that I hadn't found out more about her.

I smiled and took my seat opposite them, "So, where's the infamous Zack?" Kayleigh turned her attention to me.

"He's just running late from work," I said. I didn't know how long he'd be, so I smiled at her to show I wasn't worried. "So, Ada, where did you guys meet?" I asked.

"She came up to me in Selfridges and hit on me when I was buying makeup,"

"That makes me sound like a creep." Kayleigh rolled her eyes I laughed. "You are a creep."

Kayleigh kicked me under the table, causing Ada to giggle. "I just thought she was beautiful and wanted to tell her, what's so wrong with that?

Ada grinned. "And then we got chatting, and she asked me out for a drink." It was hard not to notice the glow on Ada's face. "She's hard to say no to."

I smiled. I liked Ada already. "Yeah, tell me about it."

A waiter came over to take our order, and quickly returned with a bottle of prosecco.

"So, Lou, Kayleigh tells me your second book will be out soon?" Ada asked, playing with her dangly jewelled earrings.

"Yeah. It's had its final round of edits now." "That's so exciting! I need to read your first one."

"You don't need to do that." I felt my cheeks heat. It was hard to sell my story to people. I never quite understood why anyone would want to read it.

"Shut up, Lou, it's brilliant. Ada can help with this year's tour wardrobe," Kayleigh interjected.

"I'd love that!" Ada squealed.

I liked the sound of that. She dressed beautifully. She was wearing a canary yellow satin dress with a high neck and puffy sleeves. It complimented her skin tone perfectly.

She clocked me looking at her outfit. “I won’t make you wear yellow, babe, don’t worry.”

We all laughed in unison. “Then you’re hired,” I joked.

“Right, where is this man of yours?” Kayleigh asked. It had been an hour, and I’d still heard nothing from him.

“I’ll ring him.” I stepped away from the table and pressed Zack’s name in my recent calls.

No answer.

Where was he?

I headed back to the table. “No signal. He must be on the tube.”

Ada smiled, “He’ll be here soon, I’m sure.” I was grateful for her optimism.

Kayleigh remained silent, watching me closely.

“So, where are you from, Ada? I sense a Brummie accent.”

I wanted to get the attention off me as quickly as possible.

I let them both lead the conversation, asking questions and laughing when required.

I had never seen Kayleigh so happy and invested in another person. She had dropped her bravado and was being attentive and kind to Ada. It reminded me of how Maeve had been with Alex when they first got together.

I kept sneakily looking at my watch to check the time. He was an hour and forty-five minutes late. He wasn’t coming. He’d let me down when I needed him not to.

“Well, I don’t think he’s coming. I bet his last client was

more work than he expected." I smiled, trying to look as unphased as possible.

"No, wait, isn't that him?" Kayleigh looked behind me.

I turned around, and low and behold, he was rushing past people to get to our table.

I breathed a sigh of relief. I didn't even care that he was late. He was here now.

"I'm so sorry, I've had a nightmare," He kissed me apologetically. "You look lovely."

"Better late than never," Kayleigh said. I looked at her to check she wasn't about ready to kill him, but she had a smile on her face and winked at me, showing me she was playing nice. "I'm Kayleigh, and this is Ada… the girl I'm… dating," Kayleigh said. I laughed. She might be monogamous, but the thought of calling anyone her girlfriend was still too much commitment.

Zack shook both their hands. "It's great to put a face to a name, Kayleigh. And it's great to meet you too, Ada."

Zack joined the table, putting his hand on mine, mouthing, *"Sorry!"* to me.

I put my hand on his and squeezed it to show it was okay.

"Late client?" Kayleigh asked. I could tell she wanted to know his excuse for even causing me a moment of distress.

"Yeah, sorry, he should have been done earlier, but it needed a lot more work to get it to look right." He looked frazzled.

"Is the shop doing well?" Kayleigh pressed.

Here we go with the interrogation.

"So far so good. We're advertising for a fifth artist to join now because of the stacked client base."

"That's so cool," Ada gushed.

Kayleigh's eyes narrowed at Zack. "So, you're not planning on leaving London anytime soon?"

"No. This is my home now." He looked at me, his lips twitching into a smile.

"That's good news." I could tell that was the answer she wanted to hear. "I'm glad it's a success."

"Thanks."

"Have you read Lou's book yet?" She pounced on the conversation before anyone could take a second to breathe.

"Not this one. She won't let me. I loved the first one so much. I bought it the day it came out."

I looked at him, surprised. I knew he had read it, but I didn't know that. We weren't even on speaking terms when it came out.

"I read it in two days," he admitted.

I wonder what Grace thought when he'd brought my book home with him…

Kayleigh didn't look impressed. "That's nice that you still supported her when you were out of each other's lives."

I darted at her with an accusatory look.

He coughed nervously. "Yes, well, I always knew she could do it, I may not have been there, but I was always rooting for her in the background."

Kayleigh harrumphed before she sat back in her chair, crossing her arms.

"Look, I know you don't like me, and you have every right not to. I'm sure you know everything I've done to Lou, and I would hate me too if I were you. But I'm here now, and I'm not going anywhere, so I hope one day you will be able to look past all of the shit I did, because I want to be a part of her life. And you are included in that." His voice was defiant.

I stared at him, shocked he'd stood up to her. Kayleigh's face was still for a moment, and then she broke into a smile. "Well, if you're here to stay, we better get another round of drinks." She looked at me approvingly.

That's all she wanted to hear, that he wasn't going to hurt me again.

The rest of the night was a blast once the awkwardness had fizzled. Kayleigh and Zack got on so well and had a lot of similar interests. She was fascinated by what it took to open a tattoo studio, and he was equally as interested in her career.

We left the bar in the early hours of the morning. Kayleigh hugged me goodbye whilst Ada and Zack hovered.

"I approve," she whispered in my ear.

"I do too," I whispered back.

My heart was full. The two people I loved most in the world liked each other, and I couldn't have been happier.

Zack and I walked into the night hand in hand after we

parted ways with Kayleigh and Ada. "I like her. She's honest, reminds me a lot of Maeve. You clearly have a type." He laughed.

I smiled. "I think that's what drew me to her. I knew she'd always have my back."

"I'm sorry I was late. You must have felt like shit, but I promised you I wouldn't let you down, and I mean it."

I stopped walking and kissed him hard. "Please don't leave me again." I sounded pathetic, but I needed him to know how I felt.

He grabbed my face in his hands and looked into my eyes. "I won't ever leave you."

Louise 2016

"Lou, can you check if table five are okay, please?" Ed called from the counter. It was a slow day at the coffee shop, just how I liked it. There were a few of the regulars in today, drinking their lattes and reading the latest bestseller, enjoying the escape from the reality of the London grind.

I had gone full time at the coffee shop after finishing university. It was a nice place to work. The owners, Ed and Marie, were a middle-aged couple who had opened the shop about seven years ago, after they'd decided kids weren't for them.

After I had finished uni, I couldn't decide what I wanted to do next. I'd had countless rejections for my book, and I was now considering what on earth I was going to do with a creative writing degree.

I thought about going into publishing, or maybe copywriting, but nothing had quite taken my fancy, until last week, when an email from a young literary agent named Kayleigh Anderson came through, saying she enjoyed my book and wanted to meet. I was shocked I had finally heard back from someone, but I knew not to get my hopes up. Not after all the rejections I'd faced. and I was happy and comfortable at the coffee shop, a true creature of habit.

I had moved into a house share down the road. It was cheap for London, and I only had to share the bathroom with one other person. Not to mention, my housemates were relatively clean, and they generally left me alone, which I appreciated.

My health had improved too. The counselling had gone from weekly to monthly check-ins. I hadn't binged and purged in over a year, and I owed it all to Jane and Maeve for helping me.

Maeve had become pretty M.I.A these days though. We'd gone from speaking all day every day to one text or a call a week. And I hadn't seen her in person for *weeks*.

She'd fallen into the party scene hard and was out constantly, especially when she knew Alex was working in the restaurant late.

This had all been going on for about two years. Her new friends were a bad influence, and it was no secret she had gotten into drugs and excessive drinking when she was around them.

I'd mentioned a few times to her that she needed to be careful, but she would just shake it off and say it was a bit of harmless fun and that I needed to relax.

The rest of the shift went fast. I read behind the counter in

between serving customers. We finally called it a day after six,
and Ed offered to lock up so I could enjoy my evening.

It was autumn, the auburn leaves crunched under my boots. It was already dark, but the streets were bright with the street lamps. There were men on forklifts putting up the Christmas decorations, turning the city into a winter wonderland.

My house was only a short walk away. I was very much in a happily confined bubble here in Brixton, with everything I needed on my doorstep. It finally felt like home.

I thought about Maeve on my walk. Maybe she was free tonight. I pulled out my phone and typed a message.

Want to hang out tonight? I miss you.

Once I got to my door, I put the key in the old lock and slightly kicked the wood to open the stiff old door.

The house was slightly run-down—hence the cheaper rent— with chipped walls, and broken furniture. It sounded like no one was in. *Perfect.* I could cook some food without being bothered.

I pressed play on my phone and let Fleetwood Mac blast before pulling ingredients out of the fridge. The music paused for a second as my phone buzzed.

Sorry babe, can't tonight! Will call soon to fill you in

on Grace and Zack's visit!

I rolled my eyes.

She had mentioned a few weeks ago that they would be coming up to visit, but it had completely slipped my mind.

I'd learnt to zone out whenever they were brought up. She kept it vague but sometimes it couldn't be helped.

I hadn't seen him since their wedding, and that's how I liked it. I'd seen on Facebook that they'd moved in together, into a new build back home, and even got a dog to complete their perfect little life.

As much as I hated her, I hoped he was treating her right. And, as much as it pained me, I did hope he was happy too.

*

The end of the week was drawing in, and my meeting with Kayleigh Anderson was now less than twenty-four hours away. I hadn't thought about it too much, it hadn't felt real… until now. I had no idea what to expect from the meeting, having never been in this situation before. I didn't know if it was a done deal that she wanted to represent me, or if she'd change her mind once we met.

What if I didn't like her? What happened then?

But then again, I was in no position to turn anyone away, and I was lucky she was even meeting me.

I took a look in the mirror at the sorry state staring back at me. I looked healthy now, but my hair hadn't quite recovered and was still lifeless and dull. My brows were overgrown, and I had a period breakout.

I rummaged through my drawer and found a facemask I had bought God knows when (and was probably out of date) but decided it was worth the risk, even finding a hair mask to add to the glow up.

I lay on my bed, hoping the masks would turn me into Megan Fox, and pulled up my manuscript on my laptop.

I couldn't remember the last time I looked at it. When editing, I'd gone over and over the same words so many times that I swear I could almost recite them by heart. But when the book was rejected. I felt rejected too, and in turn, I began to resent the whole book, and hadn't touched it since.

I knew that right now, I had to put my feelings to one side. I couldn't go to the meeting unprepared and full of disdain over my own work.

I let my old words flow through my brain, reading without coming up for air, and finally finished the book at about two in the morning.

I didn't know if it was because I was older now, or if time had healed my wound, but it felt like this was my first time reading it, and I had to admit I was pretty proud of it.

I arrived in central London mid-morning. Ed and Marie had given me the whole day off so that I could either celebrate or commiserate with some drinks, regardless of the outcome.

Maeve had texted to say she'd be on call to come and meet me afterwards.

I arrived at the address Kayleigh had given me. It was a beautiful old building that had been converted into offices.

I walked inside, admiring the architecture. I clocked the reception and was greeted by a young man with bleached blonde hair and a dangly earring.

"How can I help?" he asked, overly friendly, a customer service smile plastered on his face that I recognised in myself all too well.

"I'm Louise Moore, here to meet Kayleigh Anderson at eleven thirty."

"Great, take a seat. I will let her know you're here." He beamed a toothy grin that was slightly too white as he directed me to the waiting area.

I took a seat on a large modern orange sofa that had no business being in a building like this.

As I waited, I began to realise where I was. My leg was tapping nervously, chewing the skin around my fingers.

I felt out of control. My normal coping mechanism would be to go and make myself sick, but that was a slippery slope.

The longer I waited, the more the urge became stronger and stronger. Just as I stood up to make my way to the toilet, a voice entered the room.

"Louise?" A tall, curvy red-headed woman appeared in the

waiting room. She was wearing a matching hot pink suit that made her eyes pop from the other side of the room. I stared at her, unsure how to use my voice. I was mesmerised by how beautiful she was. "Louise Moore?" she repeated.

"Sorry, yes, sorry. I'm Louise."

Brilliant, she probably thought, "*how does a woman who can't even muster a sentence together write a book?*

She reached out and shook my hand, her nails perfectly painted and her skin soft like cashmere. "Hi, I'm Kayleigh. Follow me." She held the door open for me and led me to an office at the end of the corridor. "Come in." Directing me towards the blue velvet chair that was facing her desk.

I took a seat, and she closed the door behind her before sitting opposite me. I hadn't said anything else since confirming my identity, so my brain started working overtime, trying to string a sentence together, but no words were coming to my head.

"You're brilliant, and I'm going to make sure everyone knows it," she said confidently and passionately. "I'd love to represent you. I think there is a huge demand for fantasy books like yours at the moment, and I think I'm the person to pitch it for you. I may not have worked solely on my own book before, but you best believe I did most of the work on the ones I assisted on."

I couldn't believe how well this was going. I had come up with a full speech on why she should represent me, and I wasn't even having to use it.

"Erm, yes, I think that would be great," I sputtered.

Perhaps I was meant to act uninterested and pretend as though I was inundated with offers. Honestly, I had no idea how to play this, but I knew I already liked Kayleigh. She was bold and brash, but she put me at ease, just like Maeve.

"So, tell me, what was your inspiration? Your characters have so much depth, and Tarlin is just delicious. Please tell me he's based on someone you know?" She put her elbows on the desk and leant forward, as if she was waiting for me to tell her some salacious gossip.

"Well, I wrote it when I was nineteen, in between college and starting uni. I've kind of just been adding to it ever since." I sighed. "It has taken me a while to feel like it was finally done, though."

"Well, between you and me, I think there is a good chance we could develop this into a series. There is a lot of potential, people go wild for the fantasy genre." She sat back in her chair confidently.

My eyes widened, as did my mouth. I was in disbelief that she thought something I wrote was so good.

"Really? A whole series?" I began. "I never thought that would be possible. I wouldn't even know where to begin with a second book."

"Don't worry about that just yet. We've got time. I would like to pitch it that way, though, so have a think about whether it's something you'd like to explore." She smiled reassuringly.

I nodded. "I'm sure I could do that. Thank you."

"So, you didn't answer my question about Tarlin." She raised her brows at me.

"Well, uh, yeah. He was kind of based on a guy I knew."

"First love?"

"Yeah, I guess you could say that. How did you know?"

"People only write that beautifully about their first loves. Bitterness and cynicism haven't wormed their way in yet."

"Well, it's here now, I can assure you of that," I added with an acidic laugh.

She laughed. "You and me both, girl."

We continued chatting and getting to know each other. Kayleigh informed me that I was the first author she was representing.

I wasn't worried. I could already tell Kayleigh was someone who got exactly what she wanted, and she had a tonne of experience in publishing. I once read that it was important to gel with your agent, and I knew Kayleigh and I were destined to be friends.

I signed my contract with her there and then.

"Are you going to go and celebrate?" Kayleigh asked.

I felt elated and confident. It felt like all the pieces were finally about to slot together after so long of feeling lost.

And I knew exactly who I wanted to celebrate with.

"Yeah, with my best friend, Maeve."

"That sounds wonderful. Thank you for meeting me, Louise. I'll see you soon."

"Bye, Kayleigh, thank you so much." I walked into the corridor and pulled out my phone. I couldn't wait until I left the building to call Maeve.

"Louiseeeeee! Where are you?" Maeve answered. She was speaking loudly, and I could hear the background noise of people chatting and music blaring.

"I've been at my meeting. She's signed me, Maeve!" I continued excitedly, waiting for her reaction.

"Lou, I can't hear you," she shouted so loud I had to pull the phone away from my ear slightly.

"I'm out at an event, we are going to a party later." Her words began to slur, and she was laughing in between her words, talking to someone else in the background. "I will call you tomorrow! Love you!" She hung up before I could respond.

My heart sank. She'd forgotten all about my meeting, about my big day.

I put my back to the wall of the empty corridor and sighed. Maeve was slipping further and further away, and I wanted her back more than anything.

"Sorry, I didn't mean to interrupt, but I could hear from my office," Kayleigh emerged in the corridor out of the room. "Can your friend not make it?"

"She's had to work," I lied. I didn't need Kayleigh to know how pathetic it was that my only friend had cancelled on me for drugs.

"Come on, I'll take you out. It's a big day!" She grabbed

her bag and coat out of the office and walked towards me like a ray of light, ready to pull me out of the darkness.

Louise Present Day

"I've got to go home next week. I should only be there for a week, two at most," Zack called out from the bedroom.

I put down the spatula in my hand, turned down the hob and walked into my room. He had just gotten out of the shower, and a white towel was wrapped around his waist, his hair wet. He looked good.

I tried to focus on his face, so I didn't lose my train of thought. "What?" I asked.

"My mum's got her knee operation. Sorry, babe, I thought I'd mentioned it. I just need to help her around the house for a bit."

I racked through my memories. He hadn't mentioned it before. I was sure of it. Maybe he had just forgotten.

"Okay, well, I'll miss you." I sighed.

He noticed the frown forming on my face and pulled me

onto his lap. "Sorry, I really thought I'd mentioned it. I'll be back before you know it, promise." He pulled my hair behind my ear and kissed the side of my head. "You'll be able to concentrate on writing without me here."

"It's okay. She needs you. And yeah, you're right. I guess I could do some writing." I sat up and went back into the kitchen.

I knew it was selfish, but I was sad he was going—we hadn't spent more than a few nights away from each other in the last few months. I was also hurt that he hadn't asked me to go with him. Was he still hiding me away? Did his mum even know about me?

*

Zack went home four days ago. He'd text me to say his Mum was home and out of surgery, but not much else. I would be lying if I said I hadn't become slightly paranoid in his absence. I had another week more of this, I felt out of control, I had almost made myself sick last night, but I managed to convince myself to go on a walk to stop myself. Just like my therapist used to advise.

I hated that I was becoming so weak and pathetic again when it came to Zack. I was starting to fear that it was a feeling I'd never be able to shake so long as he was in my life.

My old wounds were re-surfacing, and I needed a distraction.

Do you want to come over later? I texted Kayleigh.

Definitely, we need some US time.

An hour later, Kayleigh arrived with a bottle of wine and some sushi in hand. She threw her arms around me as soon as she got to the kitchen.

"The dogs are away, so the cats will play," she joked.

"I don't think that's the right saying." I laughed, opening the take-out bag.

"Whatever. You get my drift."

"How's Ada and your newfound love of monogamy?" I pulled two plates out of the cupboard and dished up the food.

"Don't. I mean, she's amazing. I love being with her. But in all honesty, I'm fighting every sexual urge I have." She sighed dramatically. "Sometimes I just want to have sex with a stranger. Is that so wrong?"

"Ah, the constraints of being in love, huh?" I laughed, handing her a plate.

"Not in love! Not yet, anyway."

"Well, I like her, and I'm glad someone has finally melted your icy heart." I grinned.

"Bullshit. You're the only person who does that." She winked at me.

We both took a seat on the sofa. I began moving my chopsticks around the plate, playing with the food.

"What's wrong? Missing bae?" she teased.

"Yeah, I guess, I've not really heard from him," I muttered, hesitant to say too much. The last thing Kayleigh needed was a reason not to like Zack, especially now things between them were so positive. "He'll just be busy looking after his mum, though."

She looked at me, unconvinced. "Lou, he really will just be busy. It's not like there are loads of old girlfriends he will be meeting up with."

My face instantly dropped.

"Oh god, what did I say?"

"Grace still lives in their old house," I whispered.

I hadn't even considered the prospect that he might try to see her when he's home. I didn't know if they were still in contact or on good terms. In truth, I'd barely thought about her at all. I was too happy in my world with Zack.

I felt sick.

"Don't be ridiculous. He's going to be looking after his sick mother. Why the hell would he want to see his ex- girlfriend when he's got you at home? She's an ex for a reason."

"You're right, I'm being silly." I forced a smile.

I didn't want to share my insecurities with her. Zack had picked Grace on more than one occasion. What if he did see her? Would he change his mind and pick her again?

My mind was racing as the paranoia took over.

Kayleigh spent the rest of the night doing all the talking. I couldn't focus on what she was saying, so I just smiled and nodded along to her stories of work and her dates with Ada.

"Right, I need to go. I've got back to back meetings tomorrow." She stood up and took the plates to the kitchen. "Stop worrying. He's crazy about you, I can tell. He'll call you when he can," she said reassuringly.

When she left the apartment, I couldn't help but feel relieved that I was alone and could drop my act. I went to the bathroom and bent over the toilet.

I put my fingers in my mouth until I felt the sushi come up into my mouth.

After getting everything up, I collapsed onto the side of the bath.

I was hot and breathless, but I already felt calmer, like an old friend was holding my hand.

I knew what I had just done was wrong. I knew the shame would follow, but for now, I was grateful to have a release.

I stood up and began stripping off before getting in the shower and let the water wash away any shame. It had been a long time, but I hadn't forgotten my routine.

I jumped as I heard a loud ring. I turned off the water and frantically rummaged through the pile of clothes to try and find my phone.

I pulled it out of my jeans pocket and saw Zack's picture on my phone. I took a deep breath to try and calm down before I answered the call.

"Hey," I said.

"Hi babe, how are you?"

My heart melted, hearing his voice. "I'm good, how is your mum?"

"She's okay. It's taken a toll on her a lot more than I thought." He sighed. "Lou, I'm sorry, I know I've been shit. It's just been a lot here."

"No, it's okay. As long as you're okay." I tried to sound as calm and collected as I could.

"I know it's a big ask, but I don't think I can go much longer without seeing you. How do you feel about getting on a train and coming here?"

I beamed. I pulled the phone away, covering the microphone to squeal with excitement. I took another deep breath and returned the phone to my ear. "That sounds great. It'll be nice to see Dad too".

"Great. How early can you get here? Would tomorrow be too much of an ask? Let me know what train you're getting, and I'll pick you up from the station."

"Tomorrow works. I can't wait to see you."

He exhaled heavily, like relief had just flooded through every party of his body, and went quiet for a moment. "Thank you. I really need you."

I put the phone down and smiled to myself.

He needed me.

Louise 2016

The months had flown by since I had signed with Kayleigh. Any time that wasn't spent working at the cafe, I was with her working on the book. We had begun editing and fine-tuning the manuscript, ready to pitch to publishers.

She was the complete opposite of me; loud, opinionated and courageous. She was also flirtatious. We had many of our meetings over a glass of wine, and no one was safe from her gaze—not that anyone seemed to mind.

My relationship with Maeve had only got worse. A few texts, a call here and there. I had managed to tell her my news, and she'd promised we'd celebrate, but nothing ever came to fruition.

The Maeve-shaped void I'd felt over the last year had somewhat dissipated now that I had Kayleigh. I hadn't realised how truly alone I had been until I wasn't.

Alex had reached out to me a few times to say how worried he was getting. She had been lying to him about where she was and who she was with. Although, she hadn't realised he had clocked onto her lies.

The last time we met, I told him it was time to tell Jane and get her some help, and that we couldn't do this on our own anymore, but he begged me to give him more time to try and fix it. He knew Maeve would never forgive him if he got her mother involved.

I was on the fence. My friendship with Maeve (though distant of late) was a soul tie. Nothing would permanently break us. We could forgive anything in time. She had told her Mum about my problem, and they both had saved my life.

I wanted to do the same for her.

It was December now, the air was crisp and cold, spirits were high, and the city was magical. It was a Sunday morning at the cafe, the best day of the week to work. Young families would gather for some family time, girlfriends regroup for a post-night out debrief. I enjoyed the buzz.

I noticed a thirty-something man, handsome and blonde, tucked in a nook of the cafe that was surrounded by bookshelves. He'd been there for about an hour, making his way eagerly through a book that I wasn't close enough yet to make out. He was wearing blue jeans paired with a grey quarter zip.

He looked like he had his life together, a real grown-up.

He wasn't the usual reader-type we got here. They were

normally indie types or creatives—yet he looked more finance and corporate, which made me even more intrigued by him.

I wanted to know what he was reading, so I grabbed my pad and pen and made my way around the tables, checking if anyone needed anything, attempting to pass off my prying as just doing my job.

I noticed as I approached that he was slightly more rugged close-up, overgrown stubble and a rip in his jeans, like he didn't care as much about his appearance as I first thought. It somehow made him more appealing.

As I was about to ask him if I could get him a refill, I clocked the title of his book. '*Gone Girl*'.

Without any control, I began to laugh.

He looked up at me both with shock and amusement as soon as he realised what I was laughing at. "If you were wondering, I am indeed now terrified of you as well as the rest of the female population." His voice was deep, and his smile was kind.

"Smart choice," I giggled back to him. "He kind of deserves it, though, don't you think?"

"Absolutely. What an arrogant twit." With that answer, I knew I liked him. "I'm Chris," he held out his hand, large and veiny.

"Lou," I said, shaking his hand. "Can I get you anything else?"

"I'm okay, thank you." He paused for a moment, his eyes

searching mine, "But with the risk of being too forward, I don't suppose I can take you out some time?"

I laughed—too loudly—taken aback. When I said he wasn't my usual type, I had assumed I also wouldn't be his. Men like him didn't tend to go for messy-haired, awkward waitresses. I knew I couldn't be alone forever, I would have to date someone eventually, and maybe this one would actually want me back. I guess now was as good a time as any.

"Sure," I replied.

He handed me his book. "Write your number in there."

I looked at him, flummoxed. I had a pad in my hand. He noticed my confusion. "Put it in the book, then when we are old and grey, we've got a story of how we bonded over a sociopathic woman and an asshole man, and we will have this book to always remember it by." He sounded like he was joking, but there was definitely an undertone of seriousness in there.

I took the book from his hands and flicked through it until I found a random page near the end and wrote my number in the top corner. I then closed the book and handed it back to him.

"There, you'll have to finish the book to get the number."

"Deal. I won't contact you until I've got there fair and square. No cheating."

"Deal." I grinned.

Exactly three days later, I received a text from an unknown number.

Louise. Amy Dunn is an unsung hero. Let's have dinner to discuss? Chris (Your friendly coffee shop customer) x

We had arranged to meet the very next night. I thought he'd suggest the next week, but he seemed keen to see me.

Over the years, I had the occasional drink with men, the odd one night stand, but nothing had ever come close to Zack. I had been numb to it all since he left a gaping wound in my heart.

Chris insisted on meeting me at the tube station instead of at the movie theatre. He had booked us tickets to watch Pulp Fiction at some boutique cinema in Peckham. It was something I had always wanted to do.

I loved cinema, and didn't really have anyone I could do these things with. It had been something me and Mum used to do together when I was growing up.

We walked to the cinema, discussing our lives. He told me he worked in finance for a big corporate company in the city. He was originally from Cambridge and had moved here about ten years ago. He was incredibly interested in my book, asking me every question he could think of, not to mention telling me how he'd be going to buy it the very next day.

We spent the entire film giggling at the bad jokes he was making throughout, laughing so hard that we got disapproving looks from other customers, which made everything ten times funnier. Afterwards, he walked me back to the station and waited with me to get my tube before getting his.

"If I didn't have such a big meeting tomorrow, I'd be keeping this date going all night."

My eyes widened, not sure of his context.

He saw the horror on my face. "Oh god, no, I don't mean that. Although obviously, that would be great. No, I mean you're beautiful and funny, and I just mean I'd have liked to take you for a drink too. I don't want this date to end." He stumbled over his words, realising he was digging himself further and further into a hole.

I broke out in a fit of laughter. "You're a loser," I joked.

As gorgeous as he was, he was clumsy, cheesy, and a bit cringe. But it worked on him.

I grabbed his face with both hands and kissed him. He was stiff at first, and then relaxed into my kiss. I had never done anything so bold in my life, but I had learned the hard way that you had to take these opportunities when they arose, or you might spend the rest of your life regretting not telling someone you love them.

"Thank you for tonight," I whispered against his lips.

"You're very welcome. Let me know when you're home."

My tube approached, and he kissed me softly on the lips again.

I got on the tube and took a seat. I could see him out the window, and he began mimicking walking down the stairs.

I laughed out loud.

The rest of the carriage looked at me. I put my hand over my mouth to stifle my laugh as he continued to mime things until the tube left the station.

I couldn't remember the last time I had felt so happy, so wanted, and so full of hope for the future.

*

I shot up. My phone was ringing, I rolled over and saw that Alex was ringing me, the clock on my phone said *02:53* am.

My heart started beating fast. There was only one reason Alex would be calling me this late.

"Hello?"

"Lou! I need you," he panicked, speaking too fast. "She's not come home, and I haven't heard from her since yesterday morning. I don't know where she is."

"Alex. Calm down. I'm sure she's fine. I have her location on my phone, let me check." I pulled the phone from my ear and opened the app.

It said she was on Coldharbour Lane, last seen twenty minutes ago.

"Get an Uber to mine. She's in Brixton. I'll keep an eye on her location."

"I'm scared, Lou." His voice broke, and I could hear him holding back tears.

"It's going to be fine, Alex," I needed that to be true as

much as he did.

Alex arrived at mine half an hour later. I waited outside on the doorstep for him, refreshing my phone every minute to check she was still in the same place.

I had thrown on a pair of jeans and a giant hoodie with some old trainers, not thinking that I might be turned away from the bars dressed like this. Alex was pale, and I could tell he'd been crying. I hugged him tight before leading him down the road to begin our search.

We looked around bar after bar, praying we would find her, asking anyone who would listen if they had seen her at all. After what felt like forever, we had some luck. A young bartender told us she'd been in there earlier and that he had overheard her friends saying which bar they were going to next.

We rushed straight out and into the dark bar two doors up. The floor was sticky and the music was too loud. People looked us up and down as we walked through the crowd, clearly not dressed for the occasion.

"There she is." Alex sighed with relief. He pushed his way through the crowd of people lining up at the bar.

I heard her before I could see her. She was laughing loudly and obnoxiously. As I got closer, I could see her movements were animated and exaggerated. She was in a group of around six girls, none of whom I recognised.

Maeve was wearing a short dress, and she was flashing

the table of men opposite with each of her movements. They were looking at her like she was a piece of meat, probably discussing which one was going to try and take her home that night.

I looked at Alex, who had also clocked them. His lip quivered with rage before he worked up the courage to go over to her table.

"Maeve," he shouted over the music.

She turned around sharply and grabbed his neck, swinging her body weight on him as he tried to hold her upright. "Alex, my *lovely* husband." Her words were shrill and slurred, unrecognisable. She clocked me. "Lulu!" she screamed, heading straight for me, tripping over her heels.

"Maeve, baby. I've been so worried. Come on, let's go home," Alex pleaded.

Maeve stepped back and saw her friends watching. Her face dropped. She was embarrassed he was showing her up. She pushed his grip off her. "I'm fine." She stood up straight, trying to make herself seem sober. "I'm staying here."

"You're not fine. I haven't heard from you all day." His voice cracked. I knew he'd been pushed too far this time. "You can't keep doing this to me, Maeve. I want my wife back. Please. Let's go."

Her demeanour changed and her eyes filled with pure hatred for him. "I wish I'd never married you, Alex, you pathetic piece of shit."

Her words lingered in the air for a moment.

I looked up at Alex. I had never seen anyone's heart break in front of me until now.

"Come on, Maeve. You don't mean that," I tried to reason. "You can fuck off as well." She spat in my direction. "You can't get over some guy you liked at eight-teen, so now you're playing house with my husband, is that it?" She looked at us both like we were ruining her life. "Are you fucking him as well? Well, someone needs to, I guess." She laughed.

"Maeve," Alex pleaded.

She didn't flinch. She kept her eyes focused on me. I felt them burning through my body. I was her target now. "Who are you kidding? Little Lulu can't get any man to love her cause she makes herself sick all because her mummy died."

Instant regret flashed across her face as the words left her mouth, but she didn't move an inch, nor try to apologise. She was defiant in her rage. She just left me standing there with my wounds exposed.

She turned around and headed back to her table.

My eyes stung trying to hold back the tears. Alex grabbed my arm and led me away from her and out of the bar.

What just happened had already become a blur, the kind of blur that happens when your brain hears such an awful thing it refuses to remember it clearly to protect you. I was in shock, speechless, and on autopilot as Alex kept walking me as far away from the scene of the crime as he could.

We didn't say a word to each other the whole way back to mine. Alex walked me into the flat and sat me down on the sofa.

"Lou, I—I am so sorry." He began to cry.

His tears broke me. I tasted salt in my mouth and realised I was crying too. "Alex, you have nothing to be sorry for. She's hurt us both." I pulled him in for a hug.

"You wanted to help her a long time ago, but I was just scared that if I made her get the help, she would leave me." His breaths became sharp and fast. "I should have listened to you."

"It's okay. We'll call Jane in the morning."

He stepped away and sat down. His head fell into his hands, and he began crying harder and harder. I watched him fall apart on my sofa, and it hit me how hard this must have been for him to live with every day. I pulled his head onto me and stroked his hair to console him.

"I just want her to come back to me," he cried.

"Me too, Alex. Me too."

Louise Present Day

The train pulled into the station the next morning. I had decided to get an early train so that I didn't have to be away from Zack a moment longer than I had to. I waited by the train doors, eager to get off as fast as possible.

I practically jumped off the train and ran towards the exit. It was a small station with only two platforms, more than enough for a town this size, which I could easily navigate my way out of. I was both nervous and excited to see him. I'd missed him so much, but the reality of being a couple back in the place that had broken us so many times was intimidating. I had also never met Zack's Mum before, which added to my nerves.

In passing, Zack had met my Dad, but as nothing more than Alex's friend and nothing to do with me. I had rung him last night after speaking to Zack, letting him know I was coming home last minute, which led to me having to explain the extent of my relationship with Zack. Dad sounded a mixture of shocked, confused and pleased.

I left the station and looked around the car park, trying to spot Zack, but I couldn't see him. My stomach dropped. He said he'd meet me here. From our conversation last night, I had expected him to be waiting for me, full of excitement at the prospect of seeing me. I sighed and walked over to a small brick wall where I perched whilst I waited.

It was a cold morning. My cheeks and nose were numb where the cold pinched at my skin. I was dressed in thick tights and a black pinafore with an orange striped top underneath. I hadn't anticipated it to be this cold, so I only brought a small jacket instead of my winter coat, which I regretted the longer I was standing there.

I thought about calling him, but it had only been ten minutes. He was probably just stuck in traffic or something.

After forty-five minutes, I became increasingly annoyed. He said he needed me, yet had left
me here to freeze to death. Maybe he hadn't missed me quite as much as I'd missed him.

Somewhere in the distance, I heard a car revving up the hill into the station car park, skidding as it turned the corner. A red Fiesta pulled up right in front of me, and Zack flew out of the car to greet me, not caring that he was parked on a double yellow.

"Lou, I am so sorry I'm late." He pulled me into his chest and kissed me on the forehead. "Are you okay? Have you been waiting a long time?"

All my anger slipped away as his body warmed me. All I wanted was to get inside the car to be able to feel my toes again. "I'm okay. It's okay, don't worry," I chattered.

"You're freezing. Get in," he said, concerned, grabbing my bag from my hand and putting it in the boot as I got into the car. The car was old and loud, the seats were stained, and a lingering smell of cigarettes was embedded in the seats. Zack got in the car and saw me looking around. "Sorry, it's Mum's car."

"Don't be sorry. Not everyone can have a car as clean as yours." I remembered how oddly clean his car used to be.

He laughed. "Yeah, I loved that car so much. Lou, I am so sorry I was so late. I had to get Mum's prescription, and it wasn't ready. I just lost track of time,"

"It's okay, really. I'm just glad to see you."

"Me too. You have no idea how much I've missed you." I did have an idea, because I felt it too. "It's weird being here with you," I said. "It feels like a lifetime ago."

"Yeah, I know what you mean. It feels like two lifetimes ago."

I realised then that the last time I had lived here was before uni, but he hadn't left when I had, he'd stayed here and created a whole life for himself with Grace. He had memories here that I would never know about or understand. This town reminded me of nothing but pain, whereas it probably only reminded him of his relationship with Grace.

We remained silent for a while. He placed his hand on my thigh, and I felt the familiar electricity of his touch run through my body.

"I'm excited for you to meet my Mum. She was so happy when she knew you were coming,"

"Do you think she'll like me?" I asked.

"Absolutely. I've always seen a lot of her in you, actually."

We pulled up to the house shortly after. I had never actually been to his house before. We would always hang out at Maeve's or Alex's all those years ago, never mine or his. It was on the opposite end of town to my house. An old terrace on a quiet street, even from the outside, I could tell it had character.

All the houses on the street looked the same except this one. The door was painted black with a large brass knocker. The front garden was flowing with plants and flowers. Even in the autumn, the evergreens were bright as if it was the middle of summer. Wind chimes swayed in the window, and a welcome mat lay on the ground that said: '*Nobody's Home*'.

Zack placed his key in the lock to open the door, and I followed him in. A large wood table took over the front room with stools on either side. The walls were dark blue and had gothic style art hung around the room. A record player sat on a corner unit accompanied by an array of coloured vases.

"Wow," I gasped.

"I know. It looks like your flat, doesn't it? I told you, you're similar." He smirked at me. "Mum, we're here!" he called through the house.

He opened the door to the lounge, the walls were forest green, and two large grey chesterfield sofas were placed against either wall so that they faced the TV.

As I made my way further into the room, I saw Zack's mum sitting on the sofa.

Her leg was propped up on an ottoman. She had curly brown, almost black, hair that sat just below her shoulders. She was olive-skinned like Zack and had the same piercing blue eyes. She looked young, a lot younger than my Dad, she could only be in her mid fourties. She was very thin, especially in her face, but then I recalled how Zack had noticed my issues because he said his Mum had been through the same thing.

She turned to face us. Her eyes lit up, exposing a few wrinkles on either side, as her mouth turned into a smile. I was taken aback by how kind and warm she already appeared. "Hello, love. I'm Sam." She began to push off the sofa to lift herself.

"Oh no, don't get up," I said frantically. I took a seat next to her and held out my hand "I'm Lou."

She pushed my hand away. "Oh, none of that. I'm a hugger." And right on cue, she pulled me into her grasp. I held her back, thrilled that she was so welcoming towards me.

"I'll go make us some tea," Zack offered.

"Oh, we've got no milk left. Go get some, will you?" Sam dismissed.

"Oh, it's okay, I can get it." I was trying to be polite, but as selfish as it was, I also wanted to just be alone with Zack.

"No, it's okay. He can go. Gives us a chance to chat. " Zack looked at me, amused at how uncomfortable I probably looked. "There's a list on the fridge, you may as well do the shop whilst you're there, love."

"Okay, Mum." He kissed her on the cheek and then grabbed the list. "Won't be too long." I heard the front door shut behind him.

"He's not shut up about you all week." She turned her body so she was facing me more. "Well, in all honesty, he hasn't shut up about you in ten years, but I'm sure you know that already."

My brows furrowed in confusion. I hadn't even expected her to know who I was.

"Don't be so shocked, my love, he tells me everything. Always has."

I smiled at her, unsure how to respond without sounding narcissistic. "I didn't know you knew who I was."

"I always knew he had a soft spot for you even when he was with Grace," she paused. "He loved her, don't get me wrong, he loved her a lot." My heart quickened hearing those words.

"But they weren't good together. They didn't fit,

especially towards the end."

I winced at the thought of her knowing my involvement in the ending of their relationship.

"But when it was just him and me, he would always find a way to slip you into the conversation. He even brought me your book."

I stared at her for a moment and silence lingered between us.

"I'm sorry, I'm just a bit taken aback," I began. "I've never really talked to anyone who knows everything, and I always thought he'd forgotten about me when he met Grace, at least for the majority of it." I thought back to his drunken outburst at the wedding.

"I'm sure he tried to forget about you, but sometimes the heart has other ideas. She always kept one eye on you though." She laughed. "Sorry, not to sound awful. She was nice, just a bit full of herself. It was refreshing to see that even someone like her was insecure about someone."

"Why would she be insecure about me? He chose her afterall."

"All I know is, whenever Alex or Maeve mentioned you, she saw red."

I didn't know whether to laugh or cry that the person I had been most jealous and insecure about had felt the same way about me.

"Well, anyway, the past is in the past. They went through a

lot together, and it wasn't meant to be. And he's the happiest that I have seen him in years."

"I feel the same way." I looked at her with admiration. "You've raised a lovely man."

"Oh, don't, I'll cry. I've tried my best given the circumstances." She looked away and blinked hard.

We spent the next hour talking about our interests, she too loved horror films, and we began discussing our favourites and who the ultimate final girl was. We also had similar tastes in music, and both shared a love of Fleetwood Mac and Radiohead. It was like looking at myself in twenty years, and I liked what I saw.

Zack eventually arrived back with bags full of shopping in one hand, whilst juggling his keys and the door with the other. He got straight to work unpacking the shopping before making us both a cup of tea. We caught him up on all the things we had discovered we had in common.

"She's even better than I thought." Sam gleamed. Zack turned and winked at me.

We spent the day laughing over Zack's embarrassing childhood stories and photographs. We had some dinner and consumed several bottles of wine as we got to know each other more.

I loved seeing this version of Zack. He was so relaxed and happy around his mum, a side that not many people got to see.

Sam had sent us upstairs once she had gotten sleepy from the wine so she could go to bed. She had been sleeping downstairs since her operation as the bathroom was downstairs.

Zack's room was a dark blue, there were large stickers of artwork stuck to the matching black desk that was tucked behind the door, posters of grand theft auto and other games in large A1 frames hung over his bed. It was as if too much furniture had been crammed into the room.

He saw my expression and said, "Don't laugh. It hasn't changed since I was fifteen,"

"I can see that." I tried to hold back my laughter.

Zack closed the door behind him. He turned me around and picked me up, pulling my thighs around him. He pushed me against the wall and began to kiss me, his tongue desperately seeking mine.

"I've missed you so much," he whispered between kisses.

He pulled me from the wall and threw me onto the bed.

He took off our clothes without breaking eye contact.

He did need me. I could see it in his face.

He knelt in front of me, pulling my tights off my legs one by one, kissing my ankles and toes as my skin became exposed. He pulled up my dress and entered me. I gasped and dug my fingers into his back, letting him push against me.

We had never had sex like this before. We normally took our time, teasing with foreplay, slow and intimate, our breathing in unison, our bodies moving as one. But this was quick and rough, like we were starved of each other's touch.

We lay naked on the bed in silence, our limbs intertwined

as we regained our strength. All my worries and emotions had dissipated, and I felt safe again knowing I had him next to me. I realised, he did indeed love me as much as I loved him, whether he said it or not.

He nuzzled his head into my neck, kissing my collarbone.

"It's a true blessing to have you in my life, Louise Moore."

"Are you drunk?" I laughed.

"I am. But I mean every word of it." He turned onto his stomach and sat up slightly onto his elbows. He looked down at me intensely, and I could see the green flecks amongst the blue of his eyes. "I love you."

I took a deep breath, taking in his words.

I wanted this moment to last forever, to savour every second, to absorb my surroundings so I could replay this memory forever more.

I had waited almost ten years to hear him say that to me. It had been all I had ever wanted.

A tear fell down my cheek and onto my lips.

"I love you too," I whispered.

He kissed my lips where the tears had fallen.

The ecstasy took over, and Zack drifted to sleep, me close behind, dreaming of the moment we had just shared.

I heard a phone ping and ignored it, and then it pinged again. I was annoyed that it was disturbing my sweet thoughts.

I gently pushed Zack's arm off me and climbed out the end of the bed and round to the desk. I checked my phone.

Nothing.

I tried to find my way around the room to find Zack's trousers, so I could silence his phone. I stubbed my toe on the bedpost and stifled in a scream of pain. I found his phone in his back pocket and turned it around, ready to hit 'do not disturb', when I caught a preview of the messages on the screen.

Thanks for yesterday.
It was nice to see you.

Above the message was the name Grace.

I put my hand over my mouth so he couldn't hear my cry. I couldn't breathe. My chest felt tight, and my skin was hot.

I placed the phone back on top of his jeans and put on his shirt. I needed to get out of the room… now.

I tiptoed down the stairs, terrified I would wake up Sam. cautious of trying to stop the floorboards creaking under my weight.

I was becoming increasingly panicked. Sam was on the sofa, seemingly sound asleep. I crept past her and through the kitchen.

I slowly closed the door behind me and locked it. My breath was becoming increasingly more erratic. I reached up and opened the window, embracing the cold air on my skin and letting the fresh air fill my lungs.

The pain wasn't going away, I opened the cupboards in the

kitchen, rifling for anything I could consume. Pulling open crisp packets as fast as I could, desperate to numb the pain, hungry for the release that would come soon.

Louise 2018

"Spaghetti Bolognese or carbonara?" "Erm, surprise me!"

"Okay, sweet cheeks, I'll be home in ten."

I hung up on Chris and went to the kitchen to put the oven on. It dawned on me that we hadn't unpacked all the crockery yet, so I walked over to the lounge area and scanned the pile of boxes until I found the one that said 'kitchen stuff'.

It was right at the bottom of a four-box high tower.

Typical.

I climbed onto the arm of the sofa and reached up to the top box.

Jesus, it was heavy. What the fuck was in here?

I clumsily stepped back to the floor and placed the box down.

'*Books*'.

Seriously? What logic did we have stacking up these boxes?

I removed the other two boxes until I reached the bottom one. I grabbed my keys from the kitchen counter and sliced through the tape sealing the box together. Inside were piles of un-matching, thrifted crockery, which I had been collecting for years.

We'd lived in our own flat here for two weeks already. Kayleigh, Dad, Faye and Chris' parents had helped us move in one weekend, transporting things from our separate lives and bringing them together into our new home.

One of the only things we had that was unpacked was our Christmas tree, covered in green and gold baubles and flashing lights. It stood pride of place in our bare flat, ready for our first Christmas together in our home.

"Honey! I'm home," Chris bellowed from the hallway.

He put the Sainsbury's bag on the counter and headed over to me, where I was unwrapping the plates for us to eat off.

He planted a big kiss on my head and took them to the kitchen.

"Tell me, Chris, how did the heavy box of books end up on the top of the pile of boxes?" I teased.

"Well, Louise, we both know you're stronger than you look." He winked at me before putting a bottle of white into the fridge. "Are the glasses around too?"

"They're in that box there… I think." I pointed towards one of the boxes I retrieved earlier.

He came over and began unpacking the glasses, dancing

with them as he made his way to put them in the cupboards.

"I have a surprise for you, by the way," I said enthusiastically. I jumped up and headed into our room.

"The bedroom, huh? Is it something I haven't seen before?" he joked.

"Dream on!" I shouted from down the hall. I grabbed the cardboard box from my desk and walked back into Chris. "This came today." I handed it over to him.

"What is it?"

"Open it."

He obliged and looked inside. "No fucking way!"

"Way."

He held the book, staring at the embossed purple and red flowers on the cover, which contrasted against the matte black background and gold foiled writing: '*The Midnight Circle*.'

"Kayleigh dropped it off this morning."

"It looks incredible! How did you not explode with this news the second I walked in?"

"I wanted to surprise you." I bit my lip.

He picked me up and twirled me around until I became dizzy. "Louise Moore, you are a fucking genius. I am so proud of you." He kissed me over and over again on the cheek. My face lit up, and I let out a cackle as his kisses became ticklish.

He put me down, and I began opening the ready meal he'd bought us. I pulled back the sleeve and grabbed a fork to pierce the film.

“Did you tell Maeve?” he asked, his tone suddenly serious.

“Yeah, I texted her a picture.” I tried to avoid his eyes. “Did you hear back?”

“Alex text on behalf of them both.” I looked up quickly and saw the annoyance in his eyes. I resumed putting the garlic bread onto a tray. I didn’t want to hear it.

“Right.”

“Don’t,” I warned. Chris and I never fought unless it was about Maeve.

“I’m not. I’m sure she’ll call soon.” I could hear the insincerity etched in every word.

He knew better than to ruin this moment complaining about Maeve. I couldn’t deny we’d
drifted even further apart over the last few years, and I knew he was just protecting me, but he didn’t
know who she really was.

He had only known her since she had been sick, so he couldn’t imagine her being any different. But I knew she would get better again. Once she was back to her old self, I knew he would understand why I loved her so much.

She occasionally texted or called when she was low.

When she was drunk and out of it, she wouldn’t want to talk to me, preferring to go out and have fun. Then there were the dark stages where I wouldn’t hear from her for weeks—sometimes months—usually when she had come out of a facility or was trying to get clean.

I had felt endless guilt for not doing something to help sooner. It shouldn't have taken that fight for us to get her help. I was now haunted, looking back at all the times she'd been depressed and unwell after being out with '*work*', partying, that I just brushed off as a hangover.

At first, Alex and I thought she was just doing coke on occasion for a bit of release. She was still young, in a high-flying job, and constantly around it. It was harmless. But then it more often went to harder stuff, along with endless amounts of alcohol. We just hadn't fully realised until that night in the bar.

We called Jane as planned the very next day. She had gotten Maeve into a facility almost immediately after.

Maeve had been furious, of course. She didn't speak to Alex or me for a long time. She banned us from visiting the facility, and refused to take our calls.

Eventually, she was discharged and returned home. She turned up at my flat a few weeks later, crying her eyes out, apologising for everything she had put Alex and me through. She had promised she would never do it again and would stay clean.

It lasted about four months before she relapsed. We had been in this endless cycle of it ever since.

"Babe," Chris called. "Are you listening?"

"Sorry," I said, bringing myself back to reality. Chris filled two glasses with wine and handed me one.

"To you, Lou. A published author." We clinked our glasses together in celebration. "How cool, I get to have sex with a published author. I can't wait to tell my friends." He smirked at me.

"Well, it's a privilege, what can I say." I reached over and put my hand on his face. His jaw was strong and angular, covered in a slight amount of stubble. He was so handsome, and I was undoubtedly lucky to have someone who cared about me as much as he did.

I clocked the sunflower on my wrist as I touched his face. He saw me looking at it and kissed my wrist where it was. I pulled back my hand, feeling a twinge of guilt in my stomach. I hated that he loved part of me that wasn't his. It was a constant reminder of where part of my heart would always be.

Chris continued cooking us dinner as I unpacked some more of the kitchen boxes. We stopped to kiss one another as we navigated ourselves around the space.

I was almost done with the crockery when Chris plated the food into two bowls.

I twirled some pasta onto the fork. "I can't believe we finally live together."

"I know. It's taken us long enough. I wanted to live with you a week after meeting you," he said through mouthfuls of food.

"Oh, shut up. No, you didn't."

"I absolutely did. I knew you were the one the second you laughed at me reading gone girl. I wanted to marry you then and there."

"We aren't married, Chris."

"All in good time, my love." He winked.

Louise Present Day

I snuck back to bed once I had calmed down. I lay there still and silent, unable to sleep.

Zack was fast out cold. I looked at him. I thought I knew him so well, yet I now felt like I was lying next to a total stranger, someone who had a whole other side to them that I didn't know anything about. I tried to think of every scenario and explanation possible for Grace's message, but my mind kept going straight to the worst case.

At some point in the night, I must have drifted back to sleep, because I awoke to Zack bringing me a cup of coffee. I rubbed my eyes, trying to get them to focus.

I looked at him, placing the mug on the table next to me and sitting on the edge of the bed. My stomach was in knots.

"It's nice to have you in my bed in the morning. I feel like a naughty schoolboy," he joked whilst stroking my hair behind my ear.

I didn't know how to act. I wanted to scream at him for ruining us, but I was scared of what might unfold if I did. "I need to go see my dad today."

"Okay, can I come?"

Originally, I had wanted him there. I wanted him to meet Dad and Vicki officially, but I couldn't introduce the man who was potentially cheating on me to my family.

"I'm sure your Mum needs you here." I pulled his hand off me and sat up in bed, taking a sip of my coffee.

Zack looked at me, scrunching his brows. "Are you okay?"

I looked into his eyes, and I could see the cogs turning in his mind trying to work out if I knew. "I'm fine. I'm just going to go and take a shower."

"Okay, I'll get you a towel." He darted out of the room.

When he returned, his eyes narrowed as he handed me the towel. It was obvious he didn't want to be the first to bring it up.

I made my way downstairs. Sam was eating some toast on the sofa, watching the breakfast news.

"Morning, Lou. How did you sleep?" She was looking at me inquisitively.

"Good, thank you. I'm just going to take a shower. Do you need anything whilst I'm up?"

Her eyes narrowed, similar to the way Zack's had. She had said that he told her everything, so maybe she too was trying to work out if I knew about her son's infidelity. "No thank you, love. Feel free to use anything in the bathroom that you need." She smiled.

I stayed in the shower as long as I could, knowing that I had an uncomfortable conversation coming when I got out. I had spent my whole life avoiding confrontation as much as possible, but I knew I couldn't avoid this no matter how much I wanted to.

Eventually, I stepped out the shower, slowly brushing my wet hair behind my ears and dressing in cycle shorts and a large jumper. I didn't put any make-up on, knowing that I would inevitably cry it off.

I felt a desperation to be sick again, but I knew he'd smell it on me… and I hadn't eaten anything to throw back up anyway.

When I walked back through the house, Sam had moved into the dining room so we didn't lock eyes. I was relieved, I didn't need the pity.

Zack was waiting for me at the end of the bed. His elbows were resting on his knees. He looked up at me, and his eyes were red as if he'd been crying.

"You've seen it haven't you?" His voice was serious.

"Yes," I whispered. "I just tried to put it on silent, and it was there. I wasn't looking for it." I don't know why I felt like I had done something wrong.

"You don't need to make excuses. It's my fault."

I stayed standing, unsure where this was going. My heart was racing, terrified at what he might say.

"I can explain. Please sit down."

I sat obediently, keeping some distance between us. He

reached over to take my hand, but I pulled away. I didn't want him touching me whilst simultaneously breaking my heart.

"I know it looks really bad. There are some things you don't know that I haven't told you." He paused, trying to find his words. "Look, Grace and I were together a long time. I know we don't acknowledge the past, but I loved her, and I won't pretend that I didn't."

I winced at his words.

"What I did to her was awful. I spent years with her, living with her, planning a family with her—"

Tears began to fall from my eyes. Hearing him say how much he had loved Grace was so painful, knowing he'd wanted a family with her when he'd barely said that he loved me.

"But I lied to her. And myself. I let us both invest in our future together, but the whole time, I was thinking about you."

I looked up at him, my face scrunched up in confusion. "What do you mean?"

"I loved her, yes, but I loved you too. I've always loved you. I just didn't think I would ever be able to have you again. I didn't think I deserved you again." He looked back down at the floor in shame. "Being back with you, being so happy, I couldn't help feeling so guilty.

"So, when I knew I was coming back, I knew I needed to apologise to her. I led her on for years. I know she wasn't the nicest person, but she didn't deserve that, no one does." He looked back at me and grabbed my hands again. This time, I didn't pull away. "I should have told you. I'm sorry, but I didn't want to ruin anything. I was scared you would leave me." The tears in his eyes glistened.

I sighed, feeling confused, I knew he loved me but why was he making these stupid decisions over and over again. "I would never leave you. I have waited an eternity for this, for you. Until last night, you'd never told me you loved me. You never called it what it was until last night." "I was scared to say it."

"Why would you be scared? You knew I loved you?" I cried.

"I was scared once I said it, this would be real, and it would make you realise you were too good for me." He wiped his eyes.

"You don't want this to be real?" I asked.

"I do, I do, I swear. It's just… scary, I guess."

I put my hands on either side of his face and pulled him in so I could kiss him. I couldn't be mad any longer. We were both clearly just as insecure as each other.

And I kind of admired that he had apologised to Grace. She and Chris had been collateral damage, and we should feel guilty for the pain we had caused them.

"Lou, my feelings for you are in my bones at this point."

Knowing he had loved me all those years when I thought he had forgotten me made the heartache worth it.

"I've spent my whole life feeling like half of a person, trying to find the missing piece, and now I feel like it all makes sense.

I'm complete." He turned my wrist over and kissed the sunflower tattoo tenderly. "You are *my* sunflower."

Louise 2018

I woke the next morning bright and early, which wasn't normally like me, but I was too excited to see Kayleigh. This afternoon, we had a meeting to go over what would happen next with the book now that the final version had been approved.

There had been a soft marketing strategy happening for a few months, and it was time to push it ready for the release date that was only months away.

Kayleigh had become like a life partner in the last two years. We saw each other most days. She'd somewhat replaced Maeve in her absence, and she reminded me of her a lot. Kayleigh was a bright light in my life, and I was thankful for her every day.

I reminisced about the first day I met Kayleigh, how she entered the room just as I was about to go and make myself sick, how she'd taken me out when Maeve had forgotten all about me. She'd saved me twice that day, and she'd been saving me ever since.

I rolled over in the empty bed. Chris was already up. I climbed out of bed and went into the kitchen, where he was reading emails on his laptop.

"Coffee's still hot," he chirped.

Chris was the definition of a morning person. It normally grated on me, but I appreciated having company for my positive mood this morning.

I walked up to him and planted a kiss on his cheek.

"Remember, I'm at my work dinner tonight, babe. I'll try not to be back late," he said, knowing that I didn't like being in the flat alone at night yet. I still didn't know the area well enough, and it just felt safer with him here.

"It's okay, stay out as late as you want. I'm going to try and see Maeve."

"Are you sure?"

I wasn't sure which bit he was referring to, but I chose the less heavy option. "I'm sure, have fun."

"Okay, I'll text when I'm on my way back." He closed his laptop and put it in the case. "I should go." He leant down and kissed me tenderly on my lips. "I hope it goes okay with Maeve, call me if you need anything." I could hear the concern in his voice.

I nodded dismissively. "I love you."

"I love you too, bye." He kissed me again before he walked out the door.

*

I got to Kayleigh's office early, and she had texted to say she would be there in five minutes and to let myself in. I took a seat in the chair facing her desk, pulled out my phone and typed the name Alex into my phone.

Can I call over tonight? I know she's not her best at the moment, but I just need to see her. Let me know. Lou.

Almost immediately, my phone rang. I hit accept and put my phone to my ear.

"Sorry for the call. It's just easier," Alex began. "I think she would love to see you tonight. She's having an okay day, and she's in the best mood she's been in for weeks." Maeve had not long been home from her last stay in a facility.

"Thanks Alex. I appreciate it." I was glad she was attempting to get clean again, but I had learned by now not to get my hopes up.

"See you later."

I hung up at the same time Kayleigh waltzed into her office. "Good afternoon, my little money-maker." She handed me a takeaway coffee cup. "So, did Chris like the cover?" "He loved it. I can't wait for everyone to see it."

"I've got a few copies in that box over there for you to give to family and friends. I just wanted to wrap that one for you nicely.

It was a big moment, and you deserved something a bit more special."

"You're the world's best agent."

She grinned. "Well, duh?"

We spent the afternoon talking through what would happen over the next few weeks. I was doing a small book tour around some London bookshops, and had a few magazine and blog interviews ready for the launch.

I had ended up getting published by a big publishing house, and they'd anticipated there would be a huge market for the book within the YA fantasy community.

Kayleigh being Kayleigh, then decided I needed a new wardrobe for the events, so we went through ASOS for the rest of the meeting planning outfits.

"It's all coming tomorrow, so I'll pop over in the evening, and you can give me a fashion show,"

"Can't wait," I said sarcastically.

"You'll thank me when you see that rockin' body of yours in a pantsuit and some heels." She grabbed the box of books and handed them to me. "Don't forget these, time to go rub it in everyone's faces." She took one from the top of the box "This one's for me."

"You should rub it in everyone's face too. I couldn't have done it without you."

"Stop. I'm ginger, I can't hide when I'm blushing." She pushed me towards the door. "What are you doing with the rest of the day?"

"I'm going to go see Maeve. Give her a copy."

Kayleigh gave me a quick hug. We didn't speak much about Maeve, but she knew how much she meant to me.

"I think she'll love that. See you tomorrow."

*

It was early evening. I didn't see the point in going home first. I headed towards Tottenham Court Road and grabbed the tube to Camden, lugging around the box of books as I weaved through the crowds. I probably should have gone home first.
I got to Maeve's building and put the box on the floor to ring the buzzer.

"Come on up," Alex's voice muffled through the speaker.

I made my way up the three flights of stairs towards their flat. Alex was waiting for me in the corridor.

"She's in bed..."

I followed him in and made my way to the bedroom. The flat was normally bright white, but it felt dark and musty now. I peeped my head through the door and saw Maeve lying on the bed.

"I'll make you guys a drink."

I placed the box on the floor and sat on the bed next to her. She looked up at me and smiled.

"Lou," she croaked. "I'm so glad you're here."

"I've missed you," I muttered, stroking her hair.

Our roles had reversed entirely. She wasn't strong enough for the both of us anymore. She needed me to be the strong one.

She looked pale, her eyes dark, her hair lifeless, and her curls flat.

I went over to the box and grabbed a copy. "Here you go, I wanted you to be the first one to have it."

Maeve coughed and sat up. She held the book in her hands and began to cry. I grabbed her hands. They looked like they belonged to a seventy-year-old woman. I brought them towards my mouth and kissed her cold skin gently.

"Don't cry. It's good news."

"I'm so sorry." She looked up at me, her eyes full of tears. "I didn't even…" Her voice quivered. "I don't even remember you saying it was happening." She ran her fingers over the cover, tracing the title. "It's so beautiful."

"Read the dedication," I said.

She opened the cover and looked at the page intently.

Maeve, you are my other half, my soul mate, my person. No matter how far apart. In this life and the next, and the one after that.

Louise.

She made a noise I had never heard a human make before. It was a moan that came from her stomach, from her soul. It was as if every ounce of pain she'd felt the last few years hit her all at once.

I took the book off her and pulled her close. She leant into me, sobbing uncontrollably.

I spotted Alex at the door, holding two cups of tea. He watched as Maeve and I cried. We cried for me, we cried for her, and we cried for our friendship.

Her breaths became shallow, and her sniffling eventually stopped. She pulled away
from me and turned to get out of bed. Alex became alert, scared she'd fall.

"I'm okay." She walked over to him slowly and hugged him tightly. "I'm going to get
better. I mean it this time," she said to us both. "I don't want to miss anymore."

Alex pulled her in, and I watched as I saw a gleam of hope enter his eyes again.

Maybe she would actually get better. It seemed different this time. It seemed like it had finally gotten through to her.

We all got into bed with Maeve. She was too weak and cold to go anywhere else, but her spirits were high.

We laughed over old times, and she asked me all about Chris. I had told her a lot of the stuff before, and she'd met him many times, but she could barely remember.

We talked about our mums and how we would grow old together like they never got the chance to.

Once Maeve fell asleep, I collected my things to leave.

Alex took me to the door and hugged me. "Thank you,

Lou." His voice was croaky, holding back the tears. "We're going to get her back. I can feel it." He smiled at me through his pain.

"She never left. She just got lost." I squeezed his hand, picked up my box and headed home.

The flat was dark when I got in. Chris was still out, and I was glad he was having fun. I jumped straight in bed, snuggling into the cold sheets.

I dozed off, dreaming of all the happy memories I had with Maeve. I dreamt of us being in our eighties, laughing at our grandchildren playing together.

*

I woke up to my phone buzzing. I checked the clock, it was 3:48 am. I felt the empty bed next to me. Chris wasn't home yet, so I assumed it must be him drunk calling.

Squinting as I looked at the bright light from my phone screen, waiting for my eyes to adjust. The letters focused, and I made out the name Alex on my screen.

I stared at my phone. My heart was in my throat, and my head flashed back to earlier where Maeve was lying on her bed.

I answered the phone, and my hand shook as I brought the speaker to my ear.

"Lou—" I could hear the pain in his voice. Sobbing. "She won't wake up".

Louise Present Day

We arrived at Dad's feeling closer than we ever had before. We were united. I knew I still had to get to the bottom of Alex's comment once we were back in London, but my anxieties had subsided. I doubted there was much he could say that we wouldn't be able to get through now.

"I'm nervous," Zack whispered to me as we walked up the drive.

"Why?" I laughed. "He'll love you." That was due to the fact that Dad didn't know the history of my relationship with Zack.

I knocked on the door and waited for an answer. I hadn't seen my family for a while, and I was excited to finally make some good memories in this town.

"Hello, love," Dad said as he opened the door. He pulled me in tight and kissed me on the cheek. He stood back and took in Zack before holding out his hand to him. "Hello. I'm David."

Zack shook his hand firmly, "I'm Zack."

I couldn't help but smirk at the exchange.

We followed Dad into the house; it had become increasingly nicer over the years since Vicki had moved in. It felt like a completely separate house from the one I had left, and I was grateful for that. She had kept photos of Mum and us hung up on the walls and the mantelpiece, as well as keeping some of her ornaments and vases. She'd always kept Mum's memory alive in the house.

Vicki popped her head out the kitchen, "Hello Lou, you look lovely." She gave me a big hug. "Oh wow, what a gorgeous man," she muttered in my ear, loud enough for him to hear.

I laughed. "This is Zack,"

He greeted her sheepishly, gulping as he spoke, eyes avoiding hers. I'd never seen him look so nervous.

"Well, don't just stand there, go in the lounge. I'll get the tea, or would you prefer a coffee, Zack?"

"Tea is perfect, thank you.".

We went into the lounge, Zack and me on one sofa, and Dad on the other.

Dad crossed his legs and sat back. "So, let's cut to the chase. What are your intentions with my daughter?"

Zack's eyes widened, and he began to stutter as he looked at me.

Vicki came into the room and gave Dad a playful hit on the arm. "Oh, don't listen to him. He's just pulling your leg."

We all laughed, but Zack still looked scared.

"Sorry. It was too easy. Your face was a right picture." Zack began to laugh when he realised, he wouldn't be getting interrogated.

"Faye will be home soon. She's looking forward to seeing you."

I was glad I was going to get a chance to see her. I felt bad for Faye. I had left her here alone, forgetting that without a Mum as a teenager, she'd probably needed me a lot more than she said.

I had barely been in her life since I left. We saw each other from time to time, occasionally she would stay with me for the weekend, but we didn't text or call each other. We were more acquaintances than sisters. The afternoon was spent catching up, Dad and Zack had taken the dogs out for a walk whilst Vicki and I prepared dinner. Faye came home just before and had been filling me in on her new job at a local solicitor and the latest drama with her group of friends.

I looked at her admiringly. She had become so grown up, and I'd completely missed it. She looked exactly like Mum, with long straight brown hair, full brows and high cheekbones.

Vicki brought out a large casserole dish, placing it in the middle of the table as we all took a seat.

"Tuck in, please." She motioned before taking her seat next to Dad.

"Thank you, Vicki," Zack added.

"Not a problem, love. It's just lovely to have you both

here. We love having Louise home, and well, you're a bonus."

"We haven't seen her this happy in so long, especially since Maeve," Dad added, bowing his head to hide his sadness.

My cheeks flushed, embarrassed my misery had been so apparent. Zack put his hand on my leg under the table. "I can assure you, however happy I make her, she makes me happier tenfold."

Dad smiled. "I'm glad to hear it. She's had more loss in her life than most people her age. It's about time she got her happy ending."

"Oh, leave her alone. You're embarrassing her," Faye butted in, seeing that the flush in my cheeks had spread onto my neck.

"I'll look after her. I promise," Zack said sincerely.

I watched him as he ate his food, laughing at my Dad's jokes, asking Faye about her job, complimenting Vicki's cooking. He enamoured me. I could tell my family loved him as much as I did, and all the events of the morning melted away as I realised how lucky I was to have him in my life.

We said our goodbyes, Zack and Dad talked about going to a football match together, and Vicki gave us some leftovers to take to Zack's Mum.

Faye pulled me to one side. "I like him, Lou. He makes you happy."

I smiled and hugged her. "Please come and visit me soon. We need a girls weekend." She nodded and hugged me.

I needed to make up for the lost time.

We arrived back at Zack's on cloud nine. It had been such a big milestone for us, and it had gone better than I could have ever imagined. When we arrived back at the house, Zack went into the kitchen to reheat the food.

I took a seat next to Sam on the sofa. "It was very nice of Vicki to give me some food,"

"Oh, it's no problem. Vicki loves cooking," I assured her.

"It seems like you two had a good day,"

"It was lovely, thank you. My family loved him. He's a credit to you."

"Oh, I'm sure it's despite me," she hesitated. She gave me the look that she had given me earlier. "Listen, love. I don't mean to overstep, and you can tell me to mind my own business, but I thought I heard you in the night." She looked at me concerned and my heart sank. "I'm sure Zack's told you, but I used to suffer myself, and if you're doing it again, I'm here to talk to."

I was mortified. I had wanted to make such a good impression, but instead, she would just think of me as her son's troubled girlfriend.

"It was nothing. I just had a bit of an upset tummy, but thank you. I do appreciate the concern."

"Okay, love. I believe you, and I won't mention it to Zack." She didn't sound convinced. "But I mean it, I'm here if you need to talk."

I smiled timidly. "Thank you, but really I am fine."

“One last thing—” She lowered her voice so that I had to lean in to hear her. "I love my son, and I hope you have a long and happy life together, but if being with him brings up these urges for you in any way, you leave him. He’s wonderful, but he’s not worth that.” She leant back.

Zack entered the room right on cue. “There you go, it’s hot, be careful.”

“Thanks, son.” She smiled and began asking us about our night as if the previous conversation had never happened.

Louise 2018

I arrived at their flat with no memory of how I got there.
The flashing blue lights were all I could see as I reached the building. My body walked me up the stairs. There were people in the corridor, muffled voices speaking to me, but I couldn't make out a word they were saying.

Time was moving in slow motion. I walked through the front door, a man was speaking to me, trying to hold me back, but I pushed past him and walked into the bedroom. I could hear crying coming from the side of the room, and strangers were surrounding the bed. One person stepped back, and I saw a lifeless arm, followed by a lifeless body. She looked like she was sleeping, peaceful and pain free.

I stood there, looking down at the body in front of me. It

didn't look like her. My brain tried to take in what was happening, tried to make it seem real, but it wasn't my life. It couldn't be my life.

She'd wake up any second, laughing, telling us it was a joke.

The longer I stared at her, the more time began to move in real-time. The voices in the room became clearer. My vision became unblurred. I could see her clearly.

She was pale and grey. Her eyes were shut, her mouth slightly apart, and her skin an eerie shade of white Maeve was dead.

"We need to move her now, sir."

I turned my head, finally being able to hear what was being said.

I looked over to see Alex staring at his wife's body in thei bed, unable to respond to the paramedic trying to talk to him. Adrenaline took over my body. I snapped out of my delirium and made my way over to the paramedic. "Thank you. Does anything need signing or anything? What information do you need?"

"Thank you, miss. You are?" he asked me kindly.

"I'm Louise Moore. I'm Maeve's—" I paused, holding back the tears. "I was her best friend."

It was taking every fibre of my strength not to crumble on the spot, scream out in pain and never move again. But my brain knew how death worked. I had seen it before. This wasn't my time to crumble. I needed to stay strong for Alex because he was crumbling now.

We watched as her body was taken away. I held Alex up as he watched his wife leaving in a body bag. He was double the size of me, but I managed to lead him through to the lounge, sitting him down whilst I spoke to the police and coroner about what was to happen next.

My mum had died in hospital, so I had no idea what to do when someone died in their own home. After what felt like hours, I thanked them all for their help and closed the door behind them.

I walked into the bedroom and stripped the sheets off the bed. I didn't stop to think or take in what I was doing. I knew if I stopped for even a second to think about how my best friend had just died in these very sheets, I'd never get back up.

I put them into the washer and walked down the hall. It was dark and surreal, the only light coming from the green and red lights that flashed sporadically on the Christmas tree.

Alex was sitting exactly where I had left him, upright, not moving except for the tears streaming down his face and onto his shirt. I sat next to him, not touching him or saying a word.

Jane arrived a few hours later. She'd driven down on her own. Maeve's Dad was away on business and was arriving back in the country later that day. We heard a key in the lock, followed by her footsteps.

It was unnerving not hearing her heels. For the first time in my life, she was wearing trainers.

She came into the living area, her hair brushed back, a large jumper and leggings and not a scratch of makeup. Her eyes were bloodshot and heavy, and her skin red from her crying.

She stood in the doorway and stared at us, through us. I wasn't sure if she was going to scream at us or if she wanted to hug us. I think it was somewhere in between.

I couldn't take the silence any longer. I'd rather her shout at me than stay silent. "I'm sorry," I whispered.

Jane put her hands over her chest and took a deep breath as she let out a cry and walked towards me. "Lou, you don't have to be sorry. We did everything we could."

I stood up and hugged her tight, finally letting myself feel what I'd just been through. She held my body weight in her arms and stroked my hair as I cried so hard, I couldn't catch my breath.

I heard Alex begin to cry again behind me on the sofa.

Jane supported my body back on the sofa as she sat between us, consoling us both. I felt awful that I was letting a mother who had just lost her only child console me, but I needed my own mum more than I ever had before.

Jane was a warrior the rest of the day. She phoned everyone she needed to phone, and she even began thinking about the funeral—or at least trying to.

I watched her, admiring how strong she was. She wasn't the most affectionate woman, but she showed her love by taking care of the people around her.

When I called Chris to tell him what had happened, I

couldn't get the words out. Jane took the phone from my hands and told him that Maeve had passed. She rang my dad too. I think she knew that amongst the grief, Alex and I were in shock. We had spent yesterday afternoon filled with hope that we would get Maeve back, only to lose her the same night.

I had never known cruelty like it.

Jane told Chris to stay at the flat, and she would get me a car to get home. I was grateful. I didn't want to see him right now. I knew it wasn't his fault, but my grief was turning into anger, and I needed someone to take it out on. I hated that he had been out having fun whilst I was finding my best friend dead.

Alex and Jane were cleaning the kitchen. Jane was doing most of the talking. Alex had barely spoken all day. He just stared at her in silence, nodding his head.

His whole life had fallen apart. He was about to bury his wife at the age of twenty-six, be left alone in the city that he had only moved to for her, in a flat he had shared with her, in the bed he had found her dead in.

"We will have to do the funeral after New Year.," Jane said whilst flicking through her calendar.

Alex shot up from the table, his hands pulling at his hair.

He looked possessed.

He turned away from us and saw the Christmas tree that had continued flashing all day. He threw the tree across the room, the baubles smashing on the tile floor, the lights going dark where he had pulled them out the socket. He crouched down to the floor and sat amongst the ruins, beginning to sob.

We all looked at the destroyed tree on the floor.

Three broken hearts and one broken tree.

The next few weeks felt like I watched myself in an out- of-body experience. Alex, Jane, Chris and I travelled back home to mourn together. None of us wanted to be in the city that had played accomplice in her death. None of us wanted to be amongst the happiness of Christmas and New Year. We had no desire to watch people celebrate with loved ones. We were bitter and numb.

I was exhausted. I felt like I had been hit by a car. My limbs were heavy, as were my eyes. My brain felt full of fog, and I could barely muster a sentence together. I had cried myself to sleep every night, until one day I just had no tears left. They had run out.

Chris tried his best. He lay with me and held me through the night despite my anger still being there.

I appreciated how kind he was to me and my family. He looked after us and held us all together, but I couldn't shake my resentment. I knew he didn't love Maeve, he barely even liked her, so he was the last person I wanted to talk to.

It was New Year's Eve, and none of us felt like celebrating or even acknowledging the occasion. I spent the day lying on the sofa with Faye watching old films.

I found that wanted Faye with me most of the time.

I'd lost one sister, and I didn't want to lose another. I heard crying from the kitchen. Faye grabbed the remote and turned down the volume slightly to hear what the muffled voices were saying.

"I just feel helpless." It was Chris. Faye turned to me to gauge my reaction.

"I know. She'll come around. She's lost her Mum and her best friend in a matter of years. It's more than anyone her age should go through. I think it's just bringing up a lot of feelings for her," Dad consoled.

"I can't even imagine what she is going through. I just wish she felt she could talk to me about it."

"She bottles things up. Always has. She'll talk when she's ready,"

I looked at Faye, and she looked at me. "He's trying, you know. You need to let him in, Lou. He loves you."

"I know, I just don't know how." I chewed my lip. I felt awful that I was being so cold with him.

I was worried that if I let him in, I would lose him too. Just like Zack. Just like Maeve.

That night, I crawled into bed next to him. I burrowed myself in his chest as he wrapped his arms around me. He breathed a sigh of relief as I allowed him to get close to me.

"Thank you," I whispered, kissing his chest.

I love you so much, Louise. Whenever you're ready, I'll be here." He pulled me closer to him.

"I love you too." I kissed his chest and up to his neck, finding my way to mouth. I moved one hand into his hair, pulling slightly as I kissed him harder. I moved the other hand down his stomach and into his waistband, beginning to stroke him, feeling him get harder with my touch.

He pulled my hand away. “Are you sure?” he murmured.

I pushed my hand back onto him. “Yes.”

I was sure. I wanted him to make me forget, and I wanted anything that would help make this pain go away.

Chapter 27

Louise Present Day

We'd been back in London for a week. The rest of our visit had been a success. We spent our time going on long walks, playing board games and going for pub lunches.

Sam had begun to teach me how to knit, and I had returned with several half-finished pieces. She never mentioned our conversation again, and she was nothing but kind and loving for the rest of our stay.

I had tried to forget about the Grace thing as much as I could. Anytime I began to question it, I remembered all the things he had said to me that morning, and it pushed any doubts I had away.

"Thanks, babe." He reached up from his station, giving me a peck on the lips and taking the coffee from my hand.

We'd fallen into our new normality. It had become my

daily routine, taking him coffee or lunch at his studio.

I had finished writing my notes for the third instalment of the book, and dove head first into writing it before I lost motivation.

I walked around the studio. I liked it here. It was dark with industrial style furniture and a big leather sofa in the waiting area. The lights were dimmed to add to the atmosphere, with spotlights added around the room alongside each bed.

Two clients were getting tattooed by other artists, and the open plan made it so everyone laughed and talked to each other over the sound of music in the background.

Zack pulled me onto his lap and spun his chair around, hugging me tightly. "So, when are you going to let me tattoo you again?" He kissed my neck. "I was thinking a big 'I heart Zack' on your arm."

"Only if you get Lou tattooed on your forehead." I slapped him playfully on the head. I did want another tattoo, but I wasn't sure I wanted something that would remind me of him as much as my sunflower did. "Howabout something with an '*M*'?"

He smiled at me. "I think that's a great idea. I'll see what I can come up with." Kissing me gently, he tickled his fingers up and down my spine. His lips began tracing my ear. I could feel his breath on my neck.

"Excuse me, but we are in a professional environment." I tried to sound serious.

"I want to bend you over my desk," he whispered sternly.

"My office?"

I stood up obediently and made my way to the other side of the studio, opening the door to Zack's office. He followed behind me, telling his colleagues he had some paperwork to do.

Zack locked the door behind me. His eyes caught mine and he watched as I walked backwards. I pulled down my thong, lifted my dress and sat on his desk facing him with my legs open.

He walked towards me and began to kneel in front of me, tracing his lips along my thigh, teasing me with each kiss.

I felt his breath on me, followed by his tongue, grabbing his hair his hair, pushing his head further into me. I leaned back onto the desk, unable to keep myself up as my legs quivered from his touch.

"That feels so good," Moaning as he brought me closer to the edge.

He pulled me off the desk and turned me around, pushing me over the desk. I heard him unbutton his trousers and felt as he eased himself inside me. I could feel how hard he was for me. He began thrusting against me, pushing my head further onto the table. feeling the cold wood against my skin. I grabbed onto the edges of the desk to support myself against him as his pace quickened.

"You're so beautiful Louise, I love you," he whispered in my ear.

"I –love- you", My words broken with each thrust.

"I want you to come for me," he grunted. I came

immediately, turned on by his words. My legs shook hard as I finished, unable to support my weight. He held me in place so that he could finish inside me.

"That was amazing." He kissed my back before stepping back and redressing.

I pulled my dress down and found my knickers. "It's fun having a boyfriend with his own office," I laughed.

"It has its perks." He spanked my bum playfully. "Right, I should head back." I put my arms around his.

He looked down at me. "Thanks for my coffee… and the sex." He smiled before kissing my forehead. "Do you still want me to come tomorrow night?"

Tomorrow was the day I was supposed to help Alex clear the flat out.

We'd planned to go through Maeve's things before Zack joined us for a 'last super'.

I had pretty much all but forgotten Alex's concerns, especially after our trip, but there was still a small part of me, deep down, niggling to know what it was about.

Zack not joining us until the evening gave me ample chance to get to the bottom of it. "Yes, I do." I smiled, not giving my thoughts away. I reached up and kissed him goodbye. "See you tomorrow."

*

I arrived at the flat mid-morning. I stood outside the building for ten minutes before finally having the guts to ring the buzzer.

I heard Alex's voice come through the speaker on the door. "Doors open."

The door buzzed as it unlocked, and I headed up towards the third floor.

I opened the door to the bright white hallway. The photo frames that had been there previously were gone. There was a large gold framed mirror in its place instead.

I walked down the hallway, passing the bedroom. I kept my eyes forward so that I couldn't see inside. I made my way to kitchen. Alex was standing over the island, looking through a box of papers.

The kitchen was modern, with all high-end steel appliances against the back wall where Alex had cooked many meals for us over the years. I forgot how beautiful this flat was. Maeve's parents had helped them buy it, and it was more than anyone our age could ever dream of owning, especially in London.

I wonder how her parents felt about the flat being sold.

Alex heard me approaching and looked up.

"Weird, huh?" he said, gesturing to the large boxes filling the room's perimeters.

"Very," I replied.

"I see you're dressed for the occasion." He looked me up and down.

"Always overdressed Alex, you know me," I joked, looking down at my gym leggings paired with Zack's jumper, which practically drowned me.

"Cuppa?"

"Yeah, go on."

He turned his back to me, putting the kettle on and pulling two mugs from a half-packed box in the kitchen.

"So, I've packed the big stuff. Jane got what she wanted, so the rest is a free for all." He got some milk out of the fridge and began stirring a tea bag into the water. "I've put some pictures and stuff in a box for you to look through as well. It's on the coffee table."

Alex handed me my tea and guided me to the couch. I took a seat, pulling the box onto my lap.

My heart was racing, I reached into the box and pulled out an envelope filled with photographs. gently pulling them out, keeping my fingers on the edges. The first photo was of Maeve and me at around four years old, she was smiling up at the camera, her brilliant smile stealing the show even then. Her hair was wild and free, and she was in a yellow sundress.

She had her arm around me. I looked pale in comparison. My hair was in French plaits with bows tied at the end the way my mum had always styled my hair as a kid. I was smiling too, more shyly. Even then, the difference in our confidence was apparent.

I continued to flip through the photos. I began to cry softly, remembering the times we dressed up as witches, or made mud pies or did dance performances for our parents when we were kids.

The last photo in the pile was a candid of us from her wedding day. I traced my finger over her face. She looked so happy. I think that was the last time I had seen her like that, truly, madly happy. It had been taken when I tripped over my dress and Maeve had caught me.

"I'm always saving you, Lou," she'd laughed. We'd erupted into a fit of giggles, and the photographer had captured it perfectly.

"This was always her favourite photo," Alex whispered. "Mine too."

I looked up at him through my teary eyes. "I miss her so much." "You're telling me." He mustered a smile.

I continued looking through the box Alex had put together whilst he worked on the kitchen. There was one of her t-shirts, a snow globe I had bought her for her eleventh birthday, and a handful of cards I had written for her for various occasions over the years. She'd even kept a personalized shot glass I got her for her eighteen and an S Club 7 programme from the first concert we had gone to together.

I worked my way through the box until there was just one item left. It was my book. Well, it was my first completed copy of the manuscript I'd written. Maeve was the only person I thought would ever read the book so I'd left a note in her copy. And there it was paper clipped to the front.

My dearest Maeve,

Seeing as your best friend is an unsuccessful author who will never be published, the burden of being my book's only reader falls to you. Even if you hate it, you are obliged to pretend you don't as our love is unconditional.

Love, Lulu x

I laughed at the note, remembering how much I believed at the time that I'd never become published. If only the old me could see me now, almost three books in.

As I looked at the note, I could see ridges coming through the paper from where someone had written on the other side. I flipped it over and saw Maeve's familiar curly handwriting on the back.

My darling Lulu,

You are destined for greatness. I've always known that, and this book only cemented it for me more. One day I will give this manuscript back to you and show you this note, so you know that even when you didn't believe in yourself, I always saw the light inyou, and I always will. You are confident, beautiful, and the kindest human on this planet, and I hope by the time you read this, you already know that and don't need me to remind you.

This story is amazing, Lou. You are so talented. Your mum

wouldbe so proud of you. Now stop being a baby. The universe will make this happen for you, I'm sure of it.

Love you forever and always, M x

I sat back on the couch. I could feel the tears falling down my face. All I wanted was to hug her and say thank you for always believing in me, especially when I struggled to believe in myself.

I pulled myself together, attached the note back to the front page. The ink had smudged where my tears had fallen onto the page. I placed the manuscript back in the box along with the rest of its contents.

I somehow felt lighter. I rarely let myself think about her, and it felt nice to do so.

Alex and I worked through the flat, sorting things into 'keep' and 'donate' piles. Our emotions went from laughing over something we found, to crying only moments later.

The last thing to go through was the wardrobe. I had actively avoided going into the bedroom all day, but I couldn't escape it any longer.

The last time I was in there, she was dead; lying in the bed, pale and lifeless, surrounded by strangers. The last time I was in there, I felt an unbearable pain that I thought I would never recover from.

I took a deep breath and walked inside, taking in every inch, trying to remember all the good memories we'd had in this room—the sleepovers we had, and the laughs we'd shared.

I felt a hand on my shoulder as Alex approached the room. "I've not slept in here since. I sleep on the sofa bed," he explained with a sigh.

I looked at him, unsure what to say. He was so brave for staying in this place for as long as he did. I couldn't even imagine how many memories he made with her here. From newlyweds to a widower all before the age of thirty.

"I'm sorry I wasn't here more," I finally said.

"Don't be silly. We both did what we needed to do to survive."

We got on clearing through the bedroom in silence, words failing us as we worked through our pain.

I wiped the sweat from my forehead with the back of my sleeve and checked my watch. "Bloody hell, it's five o'clock," I said to Alex.

Zack would be here soon, and I still hadn't broached the questions I wanted to ask Alex.

"Break time, I'll get some beers." He left the room, and I could hear the fridge door open before he came back with two cold beers in hand. He handed me one and then sat on the bed, looking around at the progress we had made. "I should be able to finish the rest tomorrow,"

"Thanks for asking me to come. I think I needed this more than I thought."

"I think we both did." He patted the bed for me to sit next to him. "We need to look out for each other, Lou. She'd hate that we'd become so distant"

I stared in front of me at the almost empty wardrobe. "I know. I'm sorry, I just wasn't ready to face it all."

He put his arm around me. "I know, it's okay. I'm sorry too."

I leant into his embrace, I didn't have her anymore, but I had Alex, which was the next best thing. "Alex?" I asked. "Yeah?"

"That comment you made the last time I saw you? About Zack?"

"I was waiting for this." He sighed lightly.

"Is there something I need to be worried about?" I pulled away and looked up at him so I could read his expression.

"It's not that. It's just, Maeve would kill me if I wasn't looking out for you properly." He paused, eyeing me briefly.

"Nothing has happened, he hasn't done anything, and he is my best mate."

"Spit it out, Alex."

"He's a great guy. We love him for a reason. But we both know what he's like. He retreats as soon as anything gets serious, especially when it comes to you. I know we've never really spoken about it, but I know how much he hurt you before, and I know how unwell you got. I just don't want him to hurt you again."

He was right, just like Kayleigh was. Zack had broken me, and the people who loved me had been left to pick up the pieces.

"Do you think it's different this time?" I asked, begging for the answer I wanted to hear.

"I hope so, I really do." He pulled me back in for a hug. "If it helps, I've never seen him this happy."

"Not even with Grace?"

"No, he was never like this with Grace," he replied. "They were really serious though, Lou. More than you probably know." I felt the lump in my throat coming back. Alex stepped in before I could ask any more questions. "Look, I'm sure it will all work out."

I felt guilty for even having this conversation. Zack had proven himself to me. We were doing so well, and he was being more open with me than he had ever been before. But what did Alex mean when he said they were more serious than I knew?

I hugged Alex, thankful he was looking out for me, and I knew Maeve would have appreciated him for it as well.

Our embrace was interrupted by the buzz of the intercom. Zack was here.

Alex made his way to let him up. I looked in the mirror and made sure I was as composed as possible. I appreciated Alex's words, but I needed to live in the
moment and enjoy it for what it was. Anyway, if it didn't work out, I was strong enough now to cope.

I made my way into the hallway as Zack came through the front door. His face lit up when he saw me. He pulled me into him and buried his face in my neck.

"I missed you."

Louise 2019

It was a cold January morning. The fog was settled so low to the ground that you couldn’t see more than five feet in front of you. The air was cold and crisp, the kind of air that took your breath away.

I was sitting on the back patio of Maeve’s parents' house, letting the cold fill my lungs. I wanted to take some time to be still and alone before the day began.

Everyone was inside, getting ready to leave for the crematorium.

I knew today was the day I had to say goodbye, and the sooner I stood up and went back into that house, the sooner I would have to let her go.

I wasn’t ready to say goodbye. I wasn’t ready for life to go back to normal.

How could life ever go back to normal? How could life ever go back to normal without her?

I had never experienced this earth without her.

I thought we would have eternity. We were meant to see each other's children grow up. We were supposed to celebrate each other's fiftieth birthdays. We were supposed to face death together.

But she had left me to figure it all out on my own.

This had never been part of our plan.

I heard the French doors slide open. "It's almost time to go." Jane took a seat on the patio step beside me.

"I'm not ready." I rested my head on her shoulder.

"I know." She put her arm around me, stroking my shoulder. "The day of your Mum's funeral, I wasn't ready either."

It didn't seem fair that we had to go through this all over again. Both of us had lost two of the most important people in our lives.

"When does it get easier?"

"It doesn't get easier, but you learn to cope. Life becomes more normal again, eventually.

You start to laugh a little. You begin to let yourself love again. It all adds up, until one day you realise you aren't just surviving, you're living." She patted my knee "I've never fully healed from your mother, and I will never heal from losing Maeve. She was everything to me." She began to cry. "But I'm old, I've had my life, and I will always be a mum even without Maeve here. But you, Louise, are too young to let this kill you. You have your whole life ahead of you, so you cannot let this pain consume you. Maeve would want you to live your life to the fullest. You know that."

I wiped the tears from her cheek and smiled at her through my own. "You are a mum to me, Jane. I hope you know that."

She sniffled and wiped her eyes. 'Right, come on.

Let's go give our girl the sendoff that she deserves." Alex and I travelled in the funeral car with

Maeve's parents. They wanted us both there.

Both Jane and Maeve's father, Tony, had been unbelievably strong throughout this whole thing.

The car pulled up under the roofed driveway, right outside the crematorium doors. A sea of black surrounded the vehicles, making their way into the crematorium. As they moved, I felt their eyes burn through the tinted car window to get a glimpse of the broken people inside.

I kept my eyes focused ahead. I knew if I caught someone's gaze, the pity in their eyes would break me.

The usher opened the car door. Maeve's parents stepped out of the car first, then Alex and me. He took my hand and led me to the side to stand next to Jane.

Tony, Alex, Maeve's uncle and her cousin went to the back of the car to begin carrying the coffin. I had tried all morning not to think about it, but seeing it in person, knowing my vivacious, caring, bubbly best friend was now in a wooden box, hit me.

Jane grabbed my hand tightly using it for support as the coffin moved past us and into the crematorium.

Jane and I followed inside and took our seats in the front

row, the men following suit.

The service started, but I couldn't make out what the officiate was saying. I couldn’t take my eyes off the coffin, knowing she was in there, unable to see or feel the unbearable hole she had left in all our hearts.

I felt a nudge on my arm. I turned my head from the coffin to Alex, who was sitting to my right. “Lou, are you sure you’re okay to go up?” His eyes were filled with concern.

I was supposed to do the eulogy. I knew Alex wouldn’t be able to, and Jane had said it felt too wrong to read a eulogy for her daughter instead of the other way around, so, naturally, I offered.

I snapped back to the room. “Yes, I can do it.”

I got up from my seat, tugging my dress down as I stood. I walked up to the podium and faced the crowd.

I didn’t notice how many people were in the room until that moment. More faces than I could count staring back at me, too many for the room to accommodate. Many stood around the edge of the room.

I gulped, realising I needed to keep it together in front of all these people.

“On behalf of myself, Alex, Jane, Tony and the rest of the Winter family, we thank you all for being here today.” I could feel the lump forming in the back of my throat. I looked back into the crowd, and that's when I saw him.

He stared right at me. Our eyes locked, everyone else in the room disappeared. It was just him and me. He smiled gently, and nodded encouragingly to carry on with my speech. Instantly, I felt calm and safe.

I cleared my throat and continued reading. "Maeve Winter was a force to be reckoned with. She was a lightning bolt on this earth, a powerhouse of beauty and brains that left a mark on anyone lucky enough to have met her. My earliest memory of Maeve was when we were both four years old. A boy we went to school with had called me ugly, and I went to her crying.

"She grabbed my hand and told me that I was the most beautiful person in the whole wide world and that she would always think that even if others didn't, and then she went and smacked the boy on the head." I smiled, remembering the incident as a small laugh echoed through the crowd.

"That's who Maeve was. A protector, a supporter and an eternal optimist. Sometimes, it was hard to remember that side of her. Especially in those last few years. But her soul was always unfathomably kind and loving to the people in her life. As some of you may know, my mother was best friends with Jane. We grew up wanting to be just like them, friends, sisters, soul mates.

"It seems that, for whatever reason, history repeated itself in a way we could never imagine, and now Jane and I have to be in this world without them. But I'm sure they are up there somewhere together, laughing and dancing and taking care of each other, just as Jane and I will continue to do so down here. I hope one day we can all be reunited to make up for the lost time." A tear fell onto the paper and blurred the ink.

"To a friend, a daughter, a wife, we will miss you forever." I looked back into the crowd, straight at him.

No matter what he had done in the past, he was here. When I needed him most.

*

"I'm so proud of you for today, Lou. Your Mum would be so proud of you," Dad said once we got to the pub for the wake.

I had barely seen him all day in between doing the eulogy and accepting polite condolences from strangers.

I kissed him on the cheek lovingly, hugging him tight. He'd known Maeve her whole life, and I guess I'd been somewhat ignorant as to how hard the funeral probably was for him.

I saw Zack as he entered the pub. I hadn't gone over because he was with Grace. She was wearing sunglasses to shield her eyes. I felt a stab of annoyance that she was mourning my best friend so dramatically, but I knew Maeve would have laughed at how over the top she looked.

"I'll get us some more drinks," Chris announced. He kissed me on the head before walking to the bar. He'd been amazing today, and so patient considering how little time I was able to spend with him. I couldn't fault how supportive he had been to everyone.

"Isn't that Zack?" Faye asked me quietly.

I turned my head towards the bar to see Chris and Zack

talking whilst they waited for their drinks.

I winced. This was my worst nightmare. Chris knew nothing of Zack. For a second, Zack looked at me intensely, our eyes meeting across the room. I could feel the tension encompass me as we said a thousand words with our eyes.

Eventually, he turned to continue his conversation with Chris.

I watched them out of the corner of my eye until Chris came back over with the drinks. "That Zack guy is a bit odd," he said as he handed me my wine. "Do you know him well?"

My heart sank, I knew I needed to lie. "Not really, just through Alex." I avoided eye contact. I had never been a good liar.

Chris looked at me his browns furrowed and eyes narrow. "He seemed a bit put out when I said who I was?"

"Put out?" I scrunched my brows, feeling my heart begin to race.

"Yeah, as if he didn't like me,"

"No, not at all. We barely know each other.," I said awkwardly.

"Alright, well I don't know how Alex is mates with him, they seem so different." Chris shrugged, seemingly satisfied with my answer.

The wake was filled with polite conversations, barely listening as relatives I hadn't seen in years reminisced over Maeve. I knew she would have found it funny if she was there.

But all I thought about was her lying dead in her bed.

There wasn't enough alcohol in this pub to keep me tolerant of everyone today. I watched as people began to smile and laugh as the evening went on.

How dare they be happy today when I'd never be happy again?

I left the pub and sat outside on the bench.

Thankfully no one else wanted to be outside in the cold. I stared at an icicle

that had formed along the edge of the outhouse building, watching as it dripped slowly onto the ground.

"You shouldn't be out here." His voice travelled through my body. "It's too cold."

I looked at him as he emerged from the door. I hadn't realised how cold it was before stepping outside. I had no coat on and suddenly saw my breath in front of me. "I couldn't be in there any longer," I replied bluntly.

Zack walked over and sat next to me. "I'm not going to ask if you're okay. I won't insult you like that."

"Thank you." I was grateful he wasn't forcing me to fake it.

"I can't even imagine how you and Alex must be feeling." He paused. "I'm sorry I wasn't there for you."

"You haven't been there for me in a long time, Zack."

He winced. "I guess I deserved that. And you're right. I'm sorry. For everything."

"You should get back to Grace." I stood up to walk away.

“Wait,” he said, standing up too. He moved close to me, locking his gaze with mine.

His eyes were saying so much. His mouth opened, ready to say the words he never could, when I heard the door behind us open.

“Lou, are you okay?” I jumped, realising Chris was in the doorway watching us.

I asked myself what I was doing, why I was spending time outside with a guy who had done nothing but hurt me when I had Chris. Chris. My amazing boyfriend who had been a shoulder to cry on through the whole thing. A solid support for me and my family as we navigated another painful loss.

I looked up at Zack angrily before pushing past him and towards my boyfriend.

“Yeah, everything is fine. Just catching up.” I walked into the pub, clinging to Chris’s hand as he eyed up Zack suspiciously.

Louise Present Day

My heart was pumping, my mind racing. I re-read the message repeatedly, making sure I was reading it correctly. I opened the request to reveal the full message.

Hi Louise.
I'm sure you know by now, but Zack asked me to meet him when he was home. It cleared up a lot of things for me that I had been questioning for a long time. I'd like the chance to talk to you also. I think there are some questions we both probably need answering. Please can we meet up? I'm in London for work next week and would appreciate your time so that I can finally move on.
Grace.

I clicked off the request and immediately called Kayleigh.
"Hi Lou, you okay?"

"Hey, I need your help." "Okay?"

"So, something happened when I went home. I didn't want to tell you because I knew you'd think the worst, but Zack met up with Grace before I arrived. I found a message on his phone from her." I kept talking so that Kayleigh couldn't get a word in. "I asked him about it, and he explained that he just felt that he needed to apologise to her."

"Okay…" She sounded unsure.

"Well, I've just received a message request from her. She wants to meet up, says she needs answers. She also said that she'll answer any questions I have too."

"God. Right." She paused, thinking. "Okay. Well, I think you should hear what she has to say. You've only heard his side of the story. Don't you think you should at least hear hers too?"

I took a deep breath. "I guess."

"Lou, don't be mad at me for saying this, but do you trust Zack fully? Does any part of you
think there could be more to the story?"

"I don't know." I did know. I didn't one hundred percent trust him. Every time I did, something always came up.

I wanted to believe Zack, that it was an innocent conversation between them. I had been so happy in mine and Zack's presence, but there remained a small niggling feeling that this was all too good to be true.

"Alex told me to be careful."

"Oh."

"Yeah."

"Did he say why?"

"He just said that we both know what he's like and that Zack and Grace were really serious. I believed Zack when he said he just needed to apologise to her. And I believed Alex when he said he thought we would work out, but this message has me questioning everything."

"Lou… I know you don't want to hear it, but he doesn't have the best track record when it comes to telling you what's going on. I think you need to find out the truth for yourself beforeyou get your heart broken again."

"Do you think I'm going to get my heart broken?"

"I hope not. I hope that the guy I've got to know is who he really is."

I prayed she was right. I prayed his feelings for me were genuine, that there was nothing to worry about.

"Should I tell him she wants to meet?" I asked.

"No. Just go and meet her, or he might try to stop you. Tell him afterwards," she said sternly. "Lou, it probably is nothing, but you'll always wonder if you don't find out for yourself."

"Okay. You're right. Thank you,

Kayleigh." "I'm here for you whatever happens."

I hung up the phone and opened my messenger app backup.

Hi Grace.

Yes, I did know you both met up. I'm happy tomeet you.

Louise.

*

I spent the rest of the week trying to act as normal as possible with Zack. I tried to be as happy as I could, fully immersed in our love, but the niggle grew each day with wild ideas of what Grace would say.

My bad habits had become my escape recently, more so after this week.

Desperately consuming food whenever I was alone, I couldn't stop. The pull to binge and purge just became too intense.

"Lou? What's wrong with you at the moment? You seem distracted," he said one night whilst washing up.

"What do you mean?" I gulped, trying to compose myself, ready for the lie. "I'm fine."

"You are not fine. You've been avoiding me." He looked up from the peppers he was chopping for dinner. "Have I done something?"

"No." I smiled disingenuously. Turning to lay on the couch, staring at the ceiling. I could feel the words bubbling up through my body and towards my mouth. I had no control over it. "Did anything else happen between you and Grace when you met her?"

I heard the knife drop against the kitchen counter. I didn't want to look at him and see the look on his face.

"Why are you asking me that? It was weeks ago?" I could hear the annoyance in his voice.

"I was just wondering," I said quietly.

"I told you. I owed her an apology. I treated her terribly." He paused, waiting to see if I'd reply. "There was something that happened between us in the past, aside from you. It was hard on us both, and I needed to ask for her forgiveness."

"What did you do?" Alex had said there was something more serious between them. Grace said there were questions. I wanted to hear it from him. I wanted him to tell me his secrets so that I could go and meet Grace, fully equipped with the information I needed and to be able to trust Zack with my whole heart.

"It's between me and Grace, Louise." He only said my full name when he was being serious. "You're supposed to trust me."

I knew by his tone that I couldn't push it any further. There was no win in this situation. But I needed to know, or I would never be able to be happy with him and fully let go of our past. I would never heal and stop being this pathetic, insecure version of myself that I hated so much.

Louise 2019

The wake finally finished, and I had never been more ready to go home and take this fake smile off of my face. I left Chris downstairs with my family as they mindlessly watched TV, emotionally exhausted from the day's events. I headed upstairs to take a bath. I couldn't bear the thought of being around anyone else any longer.

The magnitude of the day, the week, and every hour I had had to live without her hit me as hard as a train storming into my body. Not to mention the added drama with seeing Zack again.

Luckily, we'd avoided eachother for the rest of the wake, only stealing glances across the room. But still, just seeing his face hurt on top of an already mounting amount of pain. I couldn't handle anymore.

I sat on the toilet seat as the water ran into the bath, the sound blocking out any noise coming from the rest of the house.

My breath became erratic, my body hot. I couldn't breathe. I grabbed a towel and screamed into it, a scream that came from the pit of my stomach.

I had just buried my best friend. My soul mate. I got in the bath, still struggling to breathe. The water was too hot. It scolded my body, but I didn't care.

I closed my eyes and immersed myself, letting the water submerge me fully.

I couldn't do it anymore. The pain was too much, and it followed me like a large cloud everywhere I went.

I opened my eyes, stinging as the water filled them. My vision blurred with just an essence of light peeking through.

A muffled noise broke through the water. My mind became clearer as I realised my phone was ringing.

I pulled myself from the water, gasping for air. I wiped my eyes and reached out for my phone, water pouring onto the floor from my arm. My intuition was screaming, telling me exactly who it was.

"Hello,"

"Lou?"

"Hi."

"I need to see you. Please."

I don't know what came over me. Maybe it was the grief,

but I didn't care about anyone or anything else in that moment, other than him. "Okay."

"I'll pick you up around the corner in fifteen minutes."

"Okay." I hung up the phone.

I stared at the tiles on the bathroom wall, watching the condensation trickle down them. My head was no longer in control of my body. My heart had gone rogue.

I pulled myself out of the bath, the water pushing against me. I barely dried myself, my hair still dripping as I walked out of the bathroom and into my room, rummaging through my closet to find a large grey hoodie and some leggings. I pulled them on and looked in the mirror. Mascara was running down my cheeks. I grabbed a wipe and removed all the reminiscence of the day from my face before heading downstairs.

I walked straight for the door when Chris appeared in the hall. "Lou? Where are you going?"

I'd forgotten he was even here. "Alex wants me to go over. "He's struggling." I lied too easily.

"Okay." He breathed. "Do you want me to come with you?"

"No, it's fine. I think it's best we just be alone tonight." I grimaced and walked over to him, placing an awkward kiss on the side of his cheek.

He watched as I walked out of the door, ignorant to where I was going.

It was icy cold out, even more so with my wet hair

clinging to my body. I walked down the drive and along the road, turning the corner at the end of the street. I was met by car headlights shining directly at me. I walked over and climbed inside, grateful for the warmth.

"Lou, where's your coat? You must be freezing," he said, pulling his coat off and putting it over me.

"Thank you," I murmured.

We drove in complete silence, but I felt relaxed and calm for the first time all day. We drove to the country park, where we had spent so much time that summer, and parked in a secluded area around the back, the trees hiding us from the world.

He shut off the engine, leaving just the heater running.

His eyes stayed staring straight ahead, watching the trees sway in the cold breeze. "I wish we could go back to that summer, sitting in this park, everything was easy."

"I don't think I've been truly happy since then," I admitted, following his eye line outside of the car.

"Me neither." We both paused.

"You were great today." He turned his head to face me.

"I'm sorry I was mean earlier. I was actually surprisingly happy to see you. Seeing your face helped me get through it. I just…" I didn't care about being vulnerable with him right now. I just wanted to say how I felt with no pretences. "I only saw you."

He smiled slightly. "They were your words, Lou. It was all you. I wish we could be here under different circumstances."

"You were the only person who knew me as she did. You

knew the dark side, the bad stuff." I breathed.

"Lou I've spent all these years thinking about you,"

"I've spent them hating you," I laughed." I could see him wince as I said the words. "But when I saw you there in the crowd, it all disappeared." I could feel a weight lifting from my shoulders. "I realised, I think I also spent them loving you, too."

"Do you love Chris?" His voice was low and serious. "Yes, but not like I loved you."

"Loved?" He turned to look at me through his lashes. "You know I still love you. I think I always will, but I'm with Chris, and you're with Grace."

"Louise, I have wondered every single day since I last saw you if you had any love for me left. You have every right to hate me, but I have hoped and prayed that some part of you still loved me… even after what I did." He moved towards me, his voice lower.

"We weren't even together, not really. How is it that something that should have been so insignificant has affected us both for so long?"

"Love doesn't have to be long to be great." He continued to move closer.

"I'm with Chris," I pleaded.

"I'm with Grace." His voice was now a whisper. He leant over and began kissing my neck. "But right now, it's you and me."

"Zack, stop." I tried to get my mind to reason with my heart, fight the desire I had for.

He pulled away ever so slightly. “Do you want me to stop?” His whisper ran through my whole body.

I shook my head, craving his touch more than I ever had before.

I succumbed to his kiss. My body was weak, I just wanted to feel nothing but him.

He rested his forehead on mine, our eyes closed, our breath synchronising. He brushed his lips against mine hesitantly before kissing me softly, slowly, pulling away between each kiss to check if it was okay.

My lips begun to move of their own accord, responding to his touch, my kisses getting deeper as his lips were moving against mine.

We removed our clothes, struggling with what little room we had in the car.

He pulled my hips towards him, my thighs around his waist, as we began to move slowly against each other.

This was right.

This is where I belonged, in his arms.

We moved faster against each other, my hand on the window for support as he moved my hips into him.

“Lou, Lou.” He moaned, biting my shoulder as we both came to a finish.

Reality came rushing back as I got back into the passenger seat. Neither of us said a word as we put our clothes back on, unsure where to go from here.

Once dressed, Zack leant his head into the steering wheel. "I'm sorry, I shouldn't have done that to you." He sighed.

"I wanted you to."

"You don't know what you want right now, Louise," he bit back.

"I want you," I whispered pathetically.

"No, you don't." His voice was cold. "I'm with Grace. I can't do this to her."

"But you have done this to her." I felt rage work its way up through my body.

"I know, and I shouldn't have." I could hear the guilt in his voice.

"No, I shouldn't have. I shouldn't have been so naïve as to think you'd finally chosen me." My voice was getting louder, breaking as tears began to fall down my face.

"Lou, I'm sorry. Don't cry." He reached out a hand to try and console me.

I pushed it off. "Don't touch me."

He pulled his hand away, looking at me with more pain in his eyes than I had ever seen.

"Don't look at me like that. Go back to Grace," I snapped, looking him dead in the eye. "I don't ever want to see you again, Zack. I mean it."

I opened the car door. My frozen tears burned my face. I began walking through the dark.

"Let me drive you home. It's too cold, Lou, please!" I heard his voice shout from the car.

I didn't turn back. I kept walking, all the way through the town, making my way back home as fast as I could. It was a wake-up call, not just from the night, but from the last few weeks.

What had I done? I had a boyfriend waiting for me at home, a boyfriend who loved me and who'd never made me feel as shitty as Zack did. A boyfriend who was with my family, helping us all to grieve. I was throwing it all away for a man who had never truly loved me, who had given up on us so easily, who had manipulated me time and time again.

I barged through the front door, wanting nothing more than to be back in Chris' arms, with a new appreciation of his love.

I walked up the stairs into my room, closing the door behind me. I saw Chris' body under the covers. I got into bed and crawled up to him, cuddling into the dip of his neck.

He held me and his breath quickened. "I saw the way you looked at him today." His voice was soft and sad. "You were with him tonight, weren't you?" The pain in his voice broke my heart all over again.

I nodded my head slowly, the tears running onto his chest. He kissed me on the forehead, his throat bobbing as he nuzzled into my hair.

We spent the night in each other's arms, and at some point, the tears sent us both to sleep.

Chris packed his stuff and left the next morning.

Louise Present Day

Zack was going out with Alex for the night, and I told him I wasgoing out with Kayleigh.

I was spiralling into a web of lies, ready to snap at any moment.

I arrived ten minutes early, wanting to get there before Grace so I could regain some of my power. I ordered a large glassof wine, hoping the alcohol would give me the courage to face her.I took a large gulp out of my glass just as Grace walked towards the table, holding some sort of fancy coloured cocktail.

She was just as beautiful as she had always been. She looked softer than she had before, less intimidating now that I knewshe'd also been concerned about me. We were the same.

She took a seat opposite me, taking a deep breath. "Sorry,I'm so nervous." She laughed awkwardly.

“Me too,” I quickly added, trying to put her at ease. “Does Zack know you’re here?”

“Not yet. I wanted to speak to you first.”

“Okay,” she added, taking a sip from her drink. “Look, I don’t know how much you know—he might have told you everything, in which case, I’ll look like a dick—but from what Zack said when we met up, I’m not sure you do, and I just think you should know our full history if you’re going to be with him again.”

“Please just tell me.” I couldn’t wait any longer. “Okay.” She sighed. “Well, I just want to make it clear that when I first met Zack, I didn’t know anything about you. He never mentioned you. I found one of his sketch pads about a year in. It was full of drawings of the same girl, as well as lots of sketches of sunflowers.”

I grabbed my wrist, recalling her comment about my tattoo at Maeve’s wedding.

“I didn’t think much of it. He drew lots of things for work, as did I. But one day, we went to Maeve and Alex’s flat. Zack wanted to introduce me to them. I stepped into their hallway, and that’s when I saw it, a framed picture of Maeve and you. The girl from the drawings.” She looked down at the table to gather her thoughts.

“I knew then that he must’ve loved you at some point, whoever you were. I never asked questions. If I’m being honest, I didn’t want to know.

As the years went on, I would hold my tongue whenever Maeve and Alex brought you up. And when I saw you and him outside at the wedding, I never even confronted him about it." She paused, watching as my face dropped. "I loved him so much, more than I knew was humanly possible. If being with him meant he occasionally reminisced about this other girl, I could do it, if I meant I had him."

I watched her, mesmerised by how this strong, beautiful woman was willing to put up with so much from a man. "I'm sorry, Grace," I whispered.

She ignored my apology and kept going. "I was at breaking point after the wedding. I saw the way he'd looked at you, he never used to look at me that way. I saw how he longed for you and how he reached for you as you walked away. I knew he wanted you more than he would ever want me. But I kept quiet, weighing up what to do next." She paused; her next words barely audible. "And then I found out I was pregnant."

My jaw dropped. I knew this was it. I knew this was the thing Zack had been keeping from me.

"We didn't plan it. I was so worried when I told him that he would think I had trapped him on purpose, that it would make him run back to you, but it didn't. He became totally invested in us, in our future. He finally started looking at me the way he had looked at you. I saw the love he had for me, for giving him the chance to be a father."

My eyes darted between hers, a million questions ran

through my head, my throat was dry and unable to speak.

"Umm, but, when we went to the twenty-week scan, the baby had no heartbeat."

"I'm so sorry." My heart broke for her and for him. "He was amazing to me at the time. I can't fault him for that. We decided to wait a while before we tried again, but we did want to. Try again. At some point. The next few years passed in bliss. You'd faded away, out of our lives—at least I thought you had. Until I found a box of your books hiding in his office. Not just one copy, but about fifteen. That's when I knew I was losing him again." She took another gulp of her drink.

"I'm not proud of this, but I told him I wanted to start trying for a baby again. I knew that was the only way to keep him, but it didn't work. We tried for two years with no luck." Her eyes welled up as she spoke. "I'm not sure why he stayed. Maybe he was just desperate for the chance to be a dad again, I don't know." She exhaled heavily. "But inevitably we began to fight. We stopped touching each other, stopped talking. We were two strangers living together.

"Then Maeve died, and selfishly I was so mad because I knew that meant he would see you again. He barely spoke to me when he found out about her. I tried to be there for him, I really did, but he completely shut me out. I knew when he snuck out the night of the funeral where he was going. I knew he had been with you when he came back smelling like a woman and unable to look at me."

Guilt ran through my veins, remembering what we had done that night.

"He tried to hide it, and I tried to get past it. And then I found out I was pregnant again." I could see the tears pooling in her eyes, threatening to spill over. She wiped them away when she noticed me looking. "It was an early miscarriage, only a few weeks in, but it still killed me. We both knew there was nothing left for us after that."

"Grace. I-I'm so sorry. I didn't know any of this." I tried to catch my breath. "I'm so, so sorry."

"I'm happy in my life now. I never expected to see Zack again until he asked to meet me. I'd waited years for him to finally tell me the truth, that he loved you and always had. And that's exactly what he did. In all honesty, I'd forgiven him long before that. He lost a lot too. He went through enough without having me hate him on top of that. He was so happy to finally have you. Seeing the way his face lit up as he spoke about you, and how happy you made him. I forgave you both when I realised that."

"I don't deserve your forgiveness, Grace."

"You know, I realised that my heart wasn't the only one that was getting broken. He'd been breaking both of our hearts over the past ten years. I don't blame you for anything. I want you to know that."

"Thank you." I smiled at her through the weight of sadness firmly planted on my chest.

"I'm sorry to have made you come out here and hear all

this, but I just wanted you to know everything so that you could make an informed decision. He isn't breaking my heart anymore, but I don't want him breaking yours, either. Although, if it's any consolation, I do believe he loves you."

It was too late, my eyes filled with tears, realising that's exactly what was happening. My heart was breaking all over again. Not just for me, but for the both of us sitting at this table.

"I'm sorry, I need to go. I need time to think." I shot up sharply from the chair.

"I understand. I hope you two can be happy together. Too many people have gotten hurt."

Louise 2019

I returned to London a week later to mine and Chris' flat. I stood outside the door, hoping that when I turned the key and opened the door, time would rewind, and he'd be sitting in the kitchen, smiling back at me.

I stepped inside. All his stuff had gone.

I walked through to the kitchen, spotting the empty spaces where his things used to be.

The Christmas tree was still up in the corner of the room. It had presents underneath it, all the ones I had bought Chris, and all the ones he'd bought me. We never got the chance to have our perfect Christmas day before the funeral.

I walked up to the tree, feeling the plastic branches between my fingers. I reached down to the plug and turned on the fairy lights, watching as they twinkled, letting them have their moment.

My eyes scanned the tree, examining the lights and ornaments. A small white envelope had been propped between the branches. I took it out and saw my name on the front, written in black pen.

I opened the envelope and pulled out a piece of paper.

Louise,

I'm sorry we couldn't make this work. I think we could have hada great life together. To be honest, that's all I've wanted since I met you. You were enough for me, and I wish I could have been enough for you. I know you've been through more than most people could ever imagine. I tried my best to be there for you, and I'm sorry if I couldn't be there for you in the way that you needed. Please know, I don't blame you. I don't hate you, and I forgive you.

I love you, and I wish you every happiness.

Chris.

I held the note to my heart, holding back the tears.

He was such a good man, so much better than me, and so much better than Zack. I hoped he would be happy with someone who deserved him one day.

I walked over to my bookshelf. It was still there, his copy of Gone Girl. I skipped the pages until I found my scrawly handwriting and slid the note inside before putting it back on the shelf.

I grabbed a bottle of wine and slumped on the sofa, not bothering to get a glass. I'd lost my best friend, my first love and my boyfriend, all in the space of a few days.

*

I spent the next four days in bed. Kayleigh had been staying in my flat since I got back to London. She was too worried to leave me on my own.

If it weren't for her, I probably wouldn't have eaten, showered or even spoken to anyone.

Here she was, saving me. Again.

"It's going to be okay. I know it doesn't feel like it right now, but the pain is temporary," Kayleigh whispered whilst spooning me in my bed.

"Kayleigh, you should go. I don't deserve you." "I'm not going anywhere."

I rolled over to face her, "I'm serious, Kayleigh. Everyone around me gets hurt, and I don't want you to be next."

She held my hands gently. "Lou, have you ever thought that maybe the people around you hurt you?"

I shook my head as I began to cry, "Not Chris, not Maeve."

"Maeve loved you. I know that, and I know she was sick, but you did nothing to hurt her. You were there for her more than most people would have been, given the circumstances. As for Chris. Yeah, he never hurt you, but he clearly wasn't right for you. Zack, however, has been hurting you pretty much ever since you met him. You've lost him, and because of him, you've lost Chris. It's time to let him go now, Lou, because that's the only thing that's holding you back."

"I know, he isn't worth it. He never was." My voice was quiet and high as I tried to speak through my tears.

"Okay, you've got until the end of the week to be as sad as you want, and then we are going to start rebuilding. You've got me, you've got your health, your family and your book. It's time to start living your life. For you."

*

It was the end of the week. Just like Kayleigh had said, it was time to rebuild. I got out of bed, changed my sheets, cooked a meal, and sat at my desk to write. Writing was who I was, it was how I could focus again.

I opened all my notes up, and began writing my second book.

Zack Present Day - Six Weeks Earlier

"It's good to see you." My voice croaked as I spoke. I began picking at a broken bit of wood hanging from the table, too uncomfortable to sit still.

"It's good to see you too, Zack. I was surprised when you reached out. I kind of thought I would never see you again."

"Yeah, I kind of thought so too." I cleared my throat. "Uh, I guess I've been doing a lot of thinking recently. A few things have been happening in my life that have made me realise that I owe you an apology." I glanced up at her to gauge her reaction, but her face was giving nothing away. "I don't have the words to say how sorry I am for how poorly I treated you over the years."

Grace paused as she digested what I was saying. "Zack." She looked into my eyes and smiled softly. "I forgave you a long, long time ago."

I let out a rush of air, relieved she was being so kind. "I wish you knew how much that means to me. I honestly thought you'd tell me to fuck off."

"Well, when two people have as much history and shared pain as we do, I'm not sure it would serve either of them to harbour any blame for the other."

"Thank you, I whispered, reaching over the table to hold her hand, stroking it with my thumb. "How are you doing?"

She squeezed my hand back. "I'm fine, you don't need to worry about me. I really am
happy. I've moved on, and—no offence—but life's easier when I'm not trying to convince
you to love me back."

I felt a twinge of guilt in my stomach. "I did love you, Grace."

"I know, but not the way you loved her." "Was it that obvious?"

She let out a stifled laugh. "To everyone but you and her. I know you think you hid it well, but you blushed anytime her name was mentioned, you had a box full of her books hidden, and, well, then there was the funeral." She turned serious as she finished her sentence.

I recalled the painful days that followed the funeral, the night Louise walked out of my car and out of my life. I had gone straight back to mine and Grace's house, ready to end it with her once and for all. I knew she knew exactly where I had been. She didn't say anything. She just looked me dead in the eye and told me she was pregnant.

I cried for hours, knowing it meant I would lose Louise forever. There was no chance I could win her back at that point. I couldn't do that to Grace or my child, not after all we'd had been through.

So, I stayed with her. I stayed with her, pretending I was happy. When, in reality, I couldn't get Louise out of my head.

We tried to make it work until the scan. When we were told there was no heartbeat, Grace and I let go of each other's hands, and we both knew there was nothing left. I probably would have stayed with her still, but she told me to go.

She set me free. And I guess she set herself free, too.

"Why are you here, Zack? What's going on?" She looked at me curiously.

"Louise." I looked down as I said her name, scared I would see the pain in Grace's eyes at my mentioning Lou's name.

When there was no reply, I looked up. A genuine, warm smile was on Grace's face, but there was a kind of sadness in her eyes. "Well, it's about time," she whispered, muffling a cry.

"I'm so sorry." I reached back for both her hands, wanting to take her pain from her. I couldn't bear the thought of causing this woman any more damage.

"Don't be sorry. I am so happy for you. I mean it. You finally got the girl you love."

My heart broke hearing her words. The reality of what I had put her through hit me like a bus.

I began to cry. Not for me, not for her… for us.

Life would have been so much easier if I had loved Grace the way that I loved Louise.

"I want you to be happy."

"I am happy, Zack. And one day, someone is going to love me the way that you love her, and when they do, I will do nothing but gloat to you," she joked through her tears.

I smiled at her, studying her. She was beautiful, bold, opinionated, brash, and, ultimately, she was kind.

"You deserve it. You deserve someone who loves you for exactly who you are. I mean that. And I'm sorry to have kept you from that for so long."

"Let's stop this crying shit now. Tell me how you two finally got together?"

"Are you sure?"

"Yes!" she exclaimed. "I'm a part of this story whether I like it or not, and I want to know how it ends."

"Well, I saw her at a bar one night. The moment I saw her standing there, I felt something in my gut. I hadn't seen her since the funeral, so I was terrified she would tell me to fuck off, but I knew I needed to try.

When I went over to her, I saw the girl I'd met at the very beginning. She seemed happy again, and I loved her just as much as I had the last time I saw her. Thankfully, she gave me a chance and let me take her out again."

"Was she worth the wait?" Grace asked.

"She was worth the wait a million times over." I couldn't

help smiling. "We are really happy."

"Has she met your mum?"

"No. I, uh… Well, I didn't ask her to come here with me."

"Why?" Grace's brows furrowed.

"Well, I don't know. I guess I just didn't want to bother her." The look on Grace's face made me realise how stupid I was being.

"Look, I don't know Louise, but I know she's just as insanely in love with you as you are with her. Do you really think she wouldn't be bothered to visit your mother with you?" she raised her brow.

"No. You're probably right."

"Do me a favour, Zack? You need to make all the pain and loss worth it. Don't fuck things up with her." She paused. "Does she know about the pregnancies?"

"No."

"You should tell her. You can't keep hiding the truth from the people you love to protect them. It doesn't work, Zack, and it's not fair. She deserves to know the full story."

I thought about Grace's words, feeling stabbing pains of guilt in my stomach. She was probably right. I should tell Louise the truth, but I needed to make sure I wouldn't lose her before I did.

"Maybe one day."

Grace sat back in her chair and smiled at me. It was a smile I hadn't seen on her face for a long time.

"Grace, I know we didn't end well, but thank you for the memories. Amongst the pain, we had a lot of happy times."

She got up from the table and walked around to where I was sitting, kissing me tenderly on the lips. "We had a good run."

Before she walked away, she turned back to me. "Tell her the truth, Zack."

Louise Present Day

I sat on the end of the bed, waiting for him to arrive. I had spent the whole night thinking about Grace's words, knowing how muchmore there was to the story, how badly he had hurt her, how badlyhe had hurt me.

I heard the key in the lock before the door opened.

"Lou?" I heard him call. His footsteps became louder as he approached my room. I looked up at him, hoping all the love and naivety would come rushing back when I looked at his face. "Louise?" He looked at my face. "What's wrong?" he froze.

"Sit down, Zack." I gestured towards the bed. "Why? What's going on?"

"Please," I practically begged.

He obliged and sat on the other end of the bed, the distance between us already growing.

"I saw Grace."

"Oh." He looked down at the floor.

"She told me everything, about the miscarriages, the books, the drawings, everything."

"I should have told you. I was going to tell you. She shouldn't have done that."

"Why didn't you tell me?"

He opened and closed his mouth a few times, as if thinking about what to say.

"I was just so scared it would push you away." I sighed. "I'm sorry for what you both went through. I can't even imagine how painful that was."

"I deserved every bit of pain."

"No, don't say that." I looked over at him, his eyes still fixed on the dark wood floor.

We sat in silence for a moment, both of us knowing the words that were about to come.

"You're breaking up with me, aren't you?"

"Yes." My voice cracked as I tried to hold back my pain. "I love you so much, Zack. I've always loved you, and I probably always will. But we hurt people, and I never realised quite how much pain we had caused until last night."

He leant down and put his head in his hands, pulling at his hair.

"We hurt Grace, we hurt Chris… and we hurt each other."

"I hurt you," he whispered. I could hear the tears in his voice. "You've never hurt me."

"That's not true. I'm hurting you now." I took a deep

breath. "Look, we can't let anyone else get hurt because of us. I think there's too much hurt from the past for us to be truly happy in the present. It shouldn't be this hard."

"Louise, please think about this. We've finally made it work, and you're just going to throw it away. All because you're mad that I didn't tell you about the miscarriages?"

"I'm not mad that you didn't tell me. I get why you didn't. I'm just disappointed you didn't want to open up to me about that part of your life. And I'm mad at us, for making Grace's pain so much worse. I'm mad that I cheated on a man who treated me with nothing but love and respect."

"I love and respect you. I know I'm not perfect, like that dickhead—"

"He's not a dickhead," I interrupted.

"Sorry. I'm just." He sighed. "I just can't lose you, Lou. I can't."

I knew I had to say it all now, or I never would get the chance again. "Zack, I've spent a decade hoping you'd realise that I was the girl you should be with. I wasted so much time praying that one day you'd wake up, come find me, and tell me I was the girl of your dreams. But you never did. And for years I kept wondering why I'd never been good enough for you."

"You are. You've always been the girl I wanted."

"I know that, I know that now. But that doesn't take away the past pain. When you finally did come and tell me those things, the damage had already been done. The insecurities were too deep-rooted to disappear. And, honestly, it shouldn't have taken you this long to realise."

"I should've left Grace so much sooner than I did," he whispered, burying his head in his hands.

"Maybe." I sigh, defeated. "But you didn't. And we are where we are. The pain is too deep rooted."

He began to cry, his anger melting. "I had no idea I had affected you so much. Please know that, with my whole heart, I think you are the most perfect creature that has ever walked this earth. Don't you let anyone, including me, ever make you doubt that again."

I nodded. "It's meant to be easier than this, Zack, and I think you know that too. This has never been easy."

He nodded and gasped for air through his tears. "I love you, Louise."

"I love you too. But right now, I need to love myself."

We looked at each other through our pain. I leant over and kissed him softly, letting the salty taste of our tears hang on our lips.

"Can I stay with you one last night?"

I nodded my head and climbed into bed, watching him get in the other side. We both lay on our sides facing each other, staring into each other's eyes as we held hands under the duvet.

"Do you think there could ever be time for us again?" He looked at me, his eyes full of pain.

"Maybe. One day. When all the pain is gone, and everyone is healed, maybe then will be our time."

"I wish we could just go back to the beginning, start over," he whispered.

"Me too."

We closed our eyes, and I ran through the memories of us. Thinking of that first summer. Laughing in the park. Falling asleep on each other in front of a film. Watching Alex and Maeve fall in love, just as we did the same.

The next morning, I woke up naturally from the sunlight trickling in. My eyes were sore and puffy from crying. I blinked as they adjusted themselves, my hands running over the sheets to find Zack.

He was already gone.

I sat up and looked around the room. It was as if he'd never been there.

I turned towards my writing desk. There was a letter propped up against my computer screen. I walked over to my desk and picked it up. Behind it was the drawing of me he had done all that time ago. I opened up the folded pieces of paper and began to read.

Zack Present Day

I stared at her. Her long lashes sweeping her cheeks, her freckles dotted over her skin, swollen from her tears. I watched as her chest rose and fell with each breath she took.

I hoped she would stay asleep as long as possible, so she didn't have to feel the pain. I wanted to stare at her sleeping for the rest of my life. But I knew that as soon as I stood up, I had to accept this was the end for us. At least for now.

I knew she was right for ending us. I knew that the pain I had put her through, put Grace through, was too much.

This was the punishment I deserved.

I didn't deserve Louise. I never had, no matter what she thought.

I knew that if I tried to persuade her to stay, I was being selfish. She needed to be free from me to be happy again. And I needed to work on facing my demons. I needed to grow up and become the man she deserved.

I knew all of this, yet I didn't say or do anything because I was selfish. And because having her love me felt too good.

Louise rolled over, turning away from me. I took that as my cue to leave. I stood up and walked over to her desk. I opened her drawers quietly, knowing it would be there somewhere.

In the bottom drawer was a big folder. I opened it, up and found a printout of an email from Kayleigh asking to be her agent, the contract for your book deal, letters from readers and a note from Maeve.

At the back of the folder, there it was, the drawing I did, my sunflower girl.

I traced my finger over her face, I always thought I was the reason for her smile, but really I was the reason for her pain, the reason she was no longer her. I put the things back into her drawer, checking sporadically to see if she was still asleep. I grabbed a pen from her pot and began writing, writing all the things I had never said.

Louise.

We both know that words have never been my strong point, and I'm not sure that I will be any better at writing them. I'm not sure where I should begin, so I guess I will start the day I met you. The first time I ever saw you, I was hooked. I wanted you the moment I laid eyes on you. You were so different and unique from anyone else I had ever met, intriguing and reserved, beautiful and mesmerising.

That summer was the happiest time of my life. I wanted to

be with you every second of every day. You were like a drug, I was so in love with you, Louise, and I was desperate for my next fix.

I'm sure you are wondering if I loved you so much, how could I let you go? Well, I did it for you, Lou. I knew that you loved me too.

I knew that if I had asked you to stay, you would have I knew we could have given it a try, but I was so relieved you were putting yourself first for once. The last thing I wanted was to hold you back. I knew being with me, having me back home, would make you want to come back and give up your dream, and I couldn't let that happen. So, I let you go.

I met Grace at work, and she asked me out. I wanted to run from my feelings for you, so I said yes. I knew you would find out; I thought it would set you free.

Seeing how you looked at me when you heard about Grace killed me. I wanted to scream at you that you were all I wanted, but I had to let you hate me so that you would walk away and become the person you wanted to be.

I learned to love Grace. That sounds cruel, I know, but it's true. Eventually, I did love her, but there wasn't a single day that went by when I didn't think about you.

The night of Maeve and Alex's wedding, I was crippled with anxiety about seeing you again. Yet, the other half of me wanted nothing more than to be in the same room as you.

I couldn't have prepared myself for how beautiful you looked. I watched you all day, smiling and laughing and enjoying your life.

Grace and I had been fighting the entire time leading up to the wedding. I was miserable, so when I saw you doing so well without me, I got drunk, and I can't remember exactly what we said to each other. But I do remember the look in your eyes. It was the same look that had been there the day you found out about Grace.

I went on the next few years, trying to forget you, letting myself be happy without you. I had made my choice, and I needed to live with it. I found out Grace and I were expecting a baby, and I knew I had to allow my heart to open for Grace fully if I was going to be half the father I wanted to be.

I can't lie to you, I loved the idea of being a dad. It made everything make sense again. When we lost the baby, Grace and I needed each other more than ever. We were going through something that only the two of us understood.

We were healing, we were trying to move on and be happy together, and then I found out about Chris. I was happy you had found someone to appreciate and love you the way you deserved.

I was happy for you, Lou. Genuinely, I was. But I couldn't stop thinking about you. I

became consumed with the thought of you again, trying to find ways of asking Maeve and Alex about you and Chris. I was desperate to know if you were happy together.

One day, I was walking around the shops on my lunch break when I saw it, I saw your book. I went straight inside to buy it, and I spent the rest of the day reading it. I had never felt so much love and pride in my entire life.

From then on, every time I saw a copy, I bought it, keeping them hidden in my office so Grace wouldn't find them.

Life kept moving. It had been almost five years since I had last seen you. I thought I would never see you again.

I committed to Grace.

Then everything changed. Maeve. Alex rang me the day after it happened, and my immediate impulse was to call you.

My heart broke for you. I wanted to be there. I wanted to be the one to console you, to pull you out of your pain. But I knew that you had Chris, and I had no right to come back and expect to be the one you wanted. You were with someone else.

When I walked into the funeral and saw you standing at the front, ready to speak, I saw you look at me, through me, and I knew that you still had some love for me somewhere. Everything I had tried to repress all those years came flooding back.

I called you that night, I wanted to see if you were okay, see if you were happy with Chris. I realise now I took advantage of you.

You had just lost your best friend, and you were vulnerable.

I honestly wanted to drive off with you and never look back. But after we did what we did, the guilt for what I had done to Grace outweighed my selfish desires for you. I didn't want to hurt her anymore.

I knew I had to end things with her, but I knew I had no right to ask you to wait for me when there was a man who loved you and was good to you right there. So, instead, I pushed you away. I pushed you away just like I always did.

I went back to Grace, ready to end things, when we found out we were pregnant again. I tried to make it work, but I couldn't get you off my mind. She lost the baby, and I knew I couldn't put her through this pain anymore. We went our separate ways, and I moved to London to start fresh.

I hoped every day that I would bump into you, and one day, I did. I knew fate had finally brought us back together that night at the bar. And I knew I couldn't mess it up this time. I was so grateful that you let me back in your life, that you could forgive me for all the pain I had caused you over the years. But here's the thing, Lou, I have been so happy to have you back in my life that I have been ignoring the fact that I am still causing you pain. Through my lack of openness and honesty, I've been making you feel insecure and alone.

I hate myself for making you feel anything less than perfect. The way you looked at me when you saw the message from Grace, it was the same look you gave me when you found out about her the first time. It was also the same look you gave me at the wedding, and the same look you gave me that night in the car. Hell, it was the same look you gave me last night.

I realised, looking in your eyes, that a hint of that pain had been in you the whole time we had been together. Every time you looked at me, it was still there.

I'm sorry I got mad. I wanted to fight for you, I really did. But then it all finally clicked in my head that, no matter how much I love you, want you and need you, I am responsible for that pain in your eyes. And, Louise, that pain will never fade whilst I am still in your life.

You deserve laugh out loud, eye twinkling, easy, painless love.

And I think we both know that I can't give you that right now. No matter how hard I try, I can't reverse the damage I have caused.

You have had so much loss and pain in your life, and I don't want to add anymore. It's not fair to you, and if I'm honest, it's not fair of me to bury my head in the sand, ignoring the glaringly obvious signs that I need to work on myself. If not for you, for myself.

You were right to end this, Louise.

You have brought me more happiness than anyone else I have ever met, and probably ever will. I am so grateful to have had you in my life at all. I WILL love you forever, no matter where life takes us. You have always been my sunflower.

Whenever life has been dark, I have looked to you to bring the light back in. I am not that person for you, and it's time you find a life full of light and happiness. I know I said this was our time, and maybe at some point it will be.

Love, Zack x

Louise One Year Later

I walked through the busy streets of London, weaving my way through the crowds of people on their way to do last-minute Christmas shopping.

I pulled my coat tight over my body, trying to keep thecold away from my chest.

My phone buzzed in my pocket. Taking my glove offand reached for my phone.

“Hey, have you seen it yet?” Kayleigh's voice sangthrough the phone, elated.

“I’m almost there.” I couldn’t hide my smile. “Send me a picture when you arrive.”

“I will. I’ll see you and Ada at seven still?”“We can’t wait. Baby included.” She laughed.

Ada’s bump was growing day by day, and Icouldn’t wait to meet her. Kayleigh and Ada were going to be the best parents.

Kayleigh was a different person, completelybesotted and

in love. Ada kept her grounded, yet softened her hard edges.

I checked my watch. Nine in the morning. Iwas right on time.

Skipping my last few steps, there it was, sat pride of place in the shop's window. My trilogy on a big display, a ‘new release’ sign next to it. I opened up my camera app and took a picture of myself with the display, forwarding it to Kayleigh, Alex, Dad, Vicki and Faye.

I turned back to look at my books, taking them in once more before heading into the shop, looking at my reflection in the window. I was no longer the sad, lonely, sick girl I was last year. I was a strong, happy and healthy woman—thanks to family, friends and a lot of therapy.

I walked inside the shop and headed for the display. Not only was my newly published third book there, but so was a special edition trilogy box set with a new limited edition white cover.

I reached for the table, flicking through the pages of my third book. It never stopped being unbelievable that my words were now printed for the world to see.

“I thought I’d be the first to buy it, but it looks like you’ve beaten me to it.” I jumped as his velvet voice penetrated my skin.

I turned around, still clutching the book. “What are you doing here?” I said, surprised.

Zack’s hair was shorter, his beard trimmed. He was wrapped in a big puffer coat, and his eyes were bright, his smile wide.

"I'm still your number one fan." He winked. My heart was full of warmth. I smiled at him, handing him the book. "Well, I can't take that title from you."

"Will you sign it first?" he asked.

I nodded, reaching for a pen in my bag. The cashier looked over at us.

"Don't worry, it's her book," he said to her with an air of unmissable pride.

I took the book from his hands and opened it to the first page.

To Zack,
My number one fan!
I genuinely never would have written this book without you pushing me to chase my dreams. You are forever in my heart and the heart of this book.
Love, your Lou. X

I closed the book and handed it back to him. He opened it up to read my words, and the corners of his eyes crinkled as he read them.

"How are you doing?" he asked, still staring at my scrawl.

"I'm really good. How are you?"

"Same."

He did look happy. He looked the best I had ever seen

him.

“I should get going,” he said. “I’m so proud of you, Louise.”

“Thanks.”

He half waved as he walked over to the cashier to pay for his book. When he finally left the shop, he turned to me and smiled before heading out into the winter air.

I picked up another copy of the book and flicked to the dedication, reading the words I knew were more true now than ever before.

You can love someone with your whole heart, but sometimes love isn’t enough. What is enough, though, is you. You are always enough. So, to that, I dedicate this book to me, to you and to anyone who has ever felt like they weren’t enough. You are enough. And more.

-Louise Moore

Maeve 2018

I watched as Louise walked out of my room, her footsteps echoing down the hallway along with the muffled voices as she said her goodbyes to Alex.

My heart ached, and my eyes stung. I rolled over to face away from the door, covering my eyes with my hand in an attempt to suppress the tears that had begun to flood out.

The tears flowed and flowed, my breathing becoming shallower as I struggled to catch enough air between sobs. I despised myself in that moment, feeling a self-loathing I had never experienced before.

I had missed the biggest moments in my best friend's life. I had missed the first years of marriage with my husband. Birthdays, holidays, work—everything important had slipped through my fingers.

It wasn't just about me; it was about everyone around me who deserved better.

But they stayed.

They showed up.

My mind raced, trying to pinpoint the exact moment when the lines blurred between harmless fun and a problem. It had all begun so innocently.

Now, here I was, grappling with the darkness that never seemed to let go. That insidious voice whispered in the depths of my thoughts, urging me towards that fix—just one more, it promised, just one more wouldn't hurt.

Desperation surged through me as I moved my hands from my eyes to my ears, attempting to silence the voice, to drown it out with anything I could muster. But it was no use; it had a hold on me that I couldn't break.

Chaos, misery, and destruction were my companions, unwelcome and yet omnipresent. The weight of the pain I had brought into the lives of those I loved bore down heavily on my conscience.

Why did they deserve this?

Why were they punished for the crime of loving me?

The door creaked open, and Alex's footsteps grew closer as he approached the bed. He slid in beside me, pulling me into an embrace until our bodies were entwined.

"I love you," he whispered gently into my ear.

My heart felt like it was shattering. "Why?" I choked out, my voice trembling.

"What do you mean, why?"

Tears traced silent paths down my cheeks as I struggled to find my words. "Why do you love me, Alex? All I've done is destroy you, us. How can you still love me after all the pain I've caused?"

I heard him take a deep breath, his chest rising and falling with the weight of his emotions. "Maeve," he said, his voice steady, "you are the kindest, bravest, sweetest, strongest person I know. I made a vow to you—a promise to stand by your side through everything. A few rough years can't change that. Do you really think I'd let this push me away?"

I rolled over to face him, meeting his bloodshot eyes. They held an intensity I hadn't seen before. "Alex," I began, my voice quivering, "our entire marriage has been a disaster. It's not just a few rough years; I've turned our life together into a living hell."

He gazed back at me, his eyes full of compassion. "Maeve," he said softly, "marriage isn't about just the easy times. It's about the shit too. And I'd rather face every storm with you than live without you.".

Tears streamed down my face as I looked into his eyes, his unwavering love and devotion piercing through me, no matter how hard I tried to push it away.

"You deserve better, Alex," I repeated, my voice trembling. "We're so young. You could start fresh, with someone who hasn't caused you pain, someone who can give you the happiness you deserve."

He held my gaze, his expression resolute. "Maeve," he

said, his voice filled with a quiet intensity, "you are all I want. You're all I need. I don't want to start again with someone else. I want to be by your side, through the good and the bad. I believe in you, and I believe in us. You can get better; I know you can."

His words wrapped around my heart like a warm embrace, shattering the walls of doubt that had kept me trapped. For the first time in a long while, a spark of hope ignited within me. "I want to," I whispered, my voice tinged with determination. "For you. And for Louise. I've been so awful to her too. How did I forget about the book? All of it?

Alex's thumb brushed away a tear from my cheek. "It's not too late, Maeve," he reassured me. "You can mend things with Louise."

"Louise has needed me, she always has. She has no one else, and I've abandoned her," I confessed, the weight of my realization pressing heavily on my heart. "She's my sister, and she's created this whole new life that I know nothing about."

Alex's arms around me tightened, his warmth a comforting anchor. "It's not too late to bridge that gap, Maeve," he assured me, his voice steady and reassuring. "Louise loves you more than anyone else on this planet. She has never given up on you, and I don't think she ever will. Neither of us will, no matter how much you try to push us away."

His words struck a chord deep within me. The idea that someone believed in me despite my faults, someone was willing to stand by me even when I couldn't see a way forward, was both overwhelming and heartwarming.

"Alex, please," I implored, my voice wavering. "I'm giving you a chance here. You can leave me, leave this misery. I won't blame you. No one will. You need to end this, because if you don't..." I took a shuddering breath, the words heavy with vulnerability. "I'm not strong enough to leave, Alex. And I can't promise you that I can get better. I want to, with all my heart, but I can't know that. And I'll never forgive myself if you stay and I end up letting you down again."

He held me close, his grip firm but gentle. His eyes bore into mine, filled with a depth of understanding that went beyond words. "Maeve," he said, his voice soft but resolute, "I'm not going anywhere. You're not alone in this battle. I choose to be here because I love you. We'll face whatever comes together."

"I love you, Alex," I whispered, my voice catching on the words.

As his arms enveloped me, I felt safe, I felt hope. Hope that I hadn't experienced in a long time.

I knew deep within my heart that this was my chance, my last chance, to make things right. To mend the destruction,

As we lay there, holding each other in the quiet embrace of the moment, I knew that I had been given another chance, a chance to make it all right.

For Alex.

For Louise.

For me.

You can find Holly Fox at these places:

WEBSITE: https://hollyfoxwrites.myshopify.com

INSTAGRAM: Hollyfoxwrites

GOODREADS: Holly

Fox TIKTOK:

Hollyfoxwrites

Reviews help authors so much so please leave a review for the book wherever you can.

ACKNOWLEDGMENTS

First and foremost, thank you to everyone who has taken the time to read my book, as a book lover myself I know how important it is to enjoy what you are reading, and so I hope you loved this book as much as I loved writing it.

The Sunflower Girl came to me when I felt like a Lou, myself not knowing if I was good enough, I wanted to write a story for all those girls. I also wanted to make a realistic love story with no big dramatic scandal but just the realisation that sometimes love isn't enough to make a relationship work and that's okay, where neither person is innocent and instead beautifully flawed.

Lou has come to mean a great deal to me, and I hope some of you can see yourself in her and know that you are good enough no matter what the scenario is. There are so many people I need to thank for helping me with my book. As a self-published author on a budget, all help has been wildly appreciated.

Firstly, I would like to thank one of my closest friends Saira who designed my cover and provided all the illustrations for the book- you completely brought my vision to life and made it a million times better. You are insanely talented and creative, and the most amazing, supportive friend and mother and I can't thank you enough.

Secondly, to my editor Paige, you were wonderful to work with; you saw my story and made it even better. You also gave me the confidence boost that I needed to let other people read it.

Next, I would like to thank all my amazing friends who have in some way helped me through this process, whether that's being my hype men, giving me confidence, supporting me or listening to me moan about how stressed I am. Fifteen years of friendship and so many more to come.

Lily, Naomi, Hannah, Alice & Olivia. - My soulmates.

Alex – my mock up man, thank you for being at the end of the phone to fix any IT things that I didn't understand no matter how busy you are!

All my wonderful friends – especially those who have brought such beautiful children into my life, constantly helping my creative brain flow.

My family for fan girling and promoting me whenever they can to whoever they can.

To my BETA and ARC readers for enjoying my story, writing reviews and promoting me, especially Gemma who understood Louise exactly as I had intended.

And lastly, to my gorgeous Godson Xander. I had always wanted to write a book but never thought I would be able to do it, and then one afternoon playing spies with Xander, my story became so elaborate someone said I should write a book- and so I did.

Milton Keynes UK
Ingram Content Group UK Ltd.
UKHW011814230823
427341UK00004B/60